***"This doesn't seem familiar," Lucas muttered, and Jocelyn froze in sudden fear.***

"What do you mean?" she asked cautiously.

"I mean shaking your hand just doesn't feel right. Not like when I talk to you. That feels natural, but shaking your hand doesn't."

"Probably because we haven't shaken hands all that often, whereas, we talk all the time," she said truthfully.

Lucas gave her a blinding smile equally mixed with devilment and relief. "Of course, I should have thought of that myself. Married couples don't go around shaking hands, do they?"

Jocelyn blinked, trying to pull her attention away from the intoxicating effect of his smile long enough to focus on what he was saying.

"Kissing would be familiar," he said softly, gently pulling her close....

Dear Reader,

The summer after my thirteenth birthday, I read my older sister's dog-eared copy of *Wolf and the Dove* by Kathleen E. Woodiwiss and I was hooked. Thousands of romance novels later—I won't say how many years—I'll gladly confess that I'm a romance freak! That's why I am so delighted to become the associate senior editor for the Silhouette Romance line. My goal, as the new manager of Silhouette's longest-running line, is to bring you brand-new, heartwarming love stories every month. As you read each one, I hope you'll share the magic and experience love as it was meant to be.

For instance, if you love reading about rugged cowboys and the feisty heroines who melt their hearts, be sure not to miss Judy Christenberry's *Beauty & the Beastly Rancher* (#1678), the latest title in her FROM THE CIRCLE K series. And share a laugh with the always-entertaining Terry Essig in *Distracting Dad* (#1679).

In the next THE TEXAS BROTHERHOOD title by Patricia Thayer, *Jared's Texas Homecoming* (#1680), a drifter's life changes for good when he offers to marry his nephew's mother. And a secretary's dream comes true when her boss, who has amnesia, thinks they're married, in Judith McWilliams's *Did You Say...* Wife? (#1681).

Don't miss the savvy nanny who moves in on a single dad, in *Married in a Month* (#1682) by Linda Goodnight, or the doctor who learns his ex's little secret, in *Dad Today, Groom Tomorrow* (#1683) by Holly Jacobs.

Enjoy!

Mavis C. Allen
Associate Senior Editor, Silhouette Romance

# Did You Say...Wife?

## JUDITH McWILLIAMS

SILHOUETTE Romance®
Published by Silhouette Books
America's Publisher of Contemporary Romance

ISBN 0-373-19681-4

DID YOU SAY…*WIFE?*



This edition published by arrangement with Harlequin Books S.A.



Visit Silhouette at www.eHarlequin.com

**Printed in U.S.A.**

**Books by Judith McWilliams**

Silhouette Romance

*Gift of the Gods* #479
*The Summer Proposal* #1562
*Her Secret Children* #1648
*Did You Say...*Wife? #1681

Silhouette Desire

*Reluctant Partners* #441
*A Perfect Season* #545
*That's My Baby* #597
*Anything's Possible!* #911
*The Man from Atlantis* #954
*Instant Husband* #1001
*Practice Husband* #1062
*Another Man's Baby* #1095
*The Boss, the Beauty and the Bargain* #1122
*The Sheik's Secret* #1228

---

## *JUDITH McWILLIAMS*

began to enjoy romances while in search of the proverbial "happily-ever-after." But she always found herself rewriting the endings, and eventually the beginnings, of the books she read. Then her husband finally suggested that she write novels of her own, and she's been doing so ever since. An ex-teacher with four children, Judith has traveled the country extensively with her husband and has been greatly influenced by those experiences. But while not tending the garden or caring for family, Judith does what she enjoys most—writing. She has also written under the name Charlotte Hines.

## Memorandum—ROUGH DRAFT

**To:** Lucas Tarrington, CEO of Tarrington Enterprises

**From:** Jocelyn Stemic

**Re:** My Resignation

Dear Mr. Tarrington,

Please let this memo serve as my official resignation. I imagine you may be shocked, but I must move on to face new challenges in my life. I did enjoy being your assistant. The only explanation I can offer for my leaving is that, well, I'm in love with you.

Sincerely,

J. Stemic

# *Prologue*

Tomorrow Lucas would be back! The knowledge warmed Jocelyn far more than the camel hair coat she was wearing. In—she checked the time on her delicate gold watch—precisely fourteen hours and twenty minutes she would see his beloved face again.

The elevator she was riding in came to a smooth stop on the ground floor, and the doors silently slid open. Automatically she headed across the broad expanse of black marble that covered the ground floor of Forester Enterprises.

''Good night, Harry.'' Jocelyn smiled happily at the elderly guard sitting behind the reception desk.

''Night, Miss Stemic.'' Harry smiled back. ''You sure look chipper. Got a heavy date tonight?''

For a brief moment an image of Lucas's leanly chiseled features filled her mind. His dark eyes glittered with emotion. His lips were curved in a sensual smile that sent her heartbeat into overdrive. What would it be like to have a date with Lucas? she wondered. To have him look at her with love and longing, instead of with his normal impersonal friendliness? It would be mind-boggling, she thought, answering her own question. World changing. Her world, at least. The closest thing to heaven on earth she was ever likely to find.

"He must really be something to send you off into a trance like that," Harry teased.

"That he is," Jocelyn agreed wholeheartedly and then hurried toward the outside doors before Harry could ask any more questions. Questions she couldn't answer. She could hardly tell him that she was head-over-heels in love with a man who viewed her as nothing more than a highly competent administrative assistant. It sounded pathetic, but it wasn't.

Just because Lucas didn't love her at the moment didn't mean that he might not come to love her in the future, she assured herself. After all, she hadn't loved him at first sight, either. When she'd interviewed for the job as his administrative assistant, she'd only thought he was incredibly sexy. It hadn't been until she'd worked with him for a few weeks that her feelings had developed into love.

It was quite possible that, given time, his liking for her might deepen enough for him to forget his determination never to become emotionally involved with a woman who worked for him. And she had time. Lots of time. Her whole lifetime.

She smiled as she shoved open the heavy, plate-glass door and caught the fragrant whiff of pine from the wreath hanging on it. It was the Christmas season, and anything was possible. Absolutely anything.

Jocelyn stepped outside, and her breath caught in her lungs as a gust of icy wind slapped her across the face. Bending her head, she hurried across the almost empty parking lot intent on getting to her car before she froze.

"Hey, babe." The irritating greeting scraped across her nerves a second before a hand closed around her upper arm. The hand jerked, pulling her against a hard masculine chest, and a man's arms embraced her.

Jocelyn instinctively tore herself out of them. She didn't want any man except Lucas hugging her.

"You can't still be mad at me, babe. Not after all these months," he said. "Hell, everyone sleeps together these days. I'm the one who should be mad. You ruined a perfectly good weekend. To say nothing of all the time I wasted dating you with nothing to show for it."

Ignoring him in the hopes he'd go away, Jocelyn pulled her remote opener out of her coat pocket and unlocked her car.

To her extreme annoyance, he hurried around the hood of her car and slipped into the seat beside her.

Jocelyn pushed back a stray tendril of her chestnut hair yanked out of the neat chignon she normally wore to work by the vicious wind, briefly wondering what Bill was doing here. She hadn't seen him in more than a year.

Deciding she didn't care enough to even ask, she said, "Get out of my car."

"Not yet. You and I need to have a talk, babe. I need help, and you're going to give it to me."

"Not this side of hell," Jocelyn said flatly.

"Oh, I think you will." His gloating expression sent a premonition of disaster through her. "You wouldn't want old Lucas to find out that his oh-so-efficient administrative assistant and the half brother he hates were lovers, now would you?"

"We weren't lovers!"

"You could try telling him that, but which of us do you think he'll believe when I show him this. Mmm?"

Bill handed her a sheet of paper.

Gingerly Jocelyn took it with a sinking feeling in the pit of her stomach—a feeling that plummeted into nausea as she read. It was the copy of a receipt for a hotel room made out in her name and Bill's. And unfortunately it was real.

Late last January he'd invited her on a skiing weekend in the Poconos. Thinking it sounded like fun, she'd agreed to go on the condition that they have separate rooms and that she pay all her own expenses. But when they'd arrived at the resort, she'd discovered that Bill had canceled her room earlier in the week and registered her into his.

Since Jocelyn had driven up from Philadelphia with Bill and the only local car rental place was closed for the night, she didn't have any way to leave. The final straw was when she had tried to get her own room and been told that the lodge was filled to capacity.

Angry and frustrated, as much at her own gullibility as at Bill's scheming, she had told Bill exactly what she thought of him. Then she had dragged half the blankets off the suite's one bed and had curled up on the couch in the sitting area to spend a very uncomfortable night. First thing in the morning she left. It had been the last time she'd seen Bill.

"How did you know I was working for Lucas?" she said, trying to give herself time to think.

"Dear cousin Emmy. She was bragging about how she'd helped you find the job as old Lucas's administrative assistant."

"But why contact me now? I've had this job for six months."

"Because I've suffered a few financial reverses."

Bill shoved his fingers through his perfectly barbered hair. "To put it bluntly, I've spent every penny Dad left me, and if I can't find a new source of income—"

"You'll have to go to work like the rest of us?" she said unsympathetically. "Blackmailing me won't help you. My entire life's savings wouldn't keep you for a week."

"Not you, you stupid witch! Lucas."

Jocelyn grimaced. "Surely you can't think I have his power of attorney?"

"You always did think small," he said coldly. "I don't want to embezzle from the company. I want to *take over* the company. I can sell it for a fortune. It should have been mine, anyway."

"Lucas's father left it to him." Jocelyn repeated what Emmy had told her.

"I think Lucas substituted a fake will for the real one. Mom does, too."

Jocelyn watched as his mouth suddenly compressed, giving him a mean, vicious look, and she shivered, glad they were in an open parking lot in full view of any passersby.

"Has it occurred to either of you that Lucas's father might not have had any choice but to leave the company to Lucas?" Jocelyn said. "From what Emmy said, the company originally belonged to Lucas's mother. Maybe it was—" she gestured ineffectively "—whatever the modern-day equivalent of an entail is?"

"Not a chance. Mom was very careful to look up Dad's first wife's will before she married him. Lucas's mother left everything she owned to her husband. No, the only explanation for why Dad didn't leave the company to me was because Lucas substituted a fake will. And I want you to help me find the real one."

"Use your head, Bill," Jocelyn tried to reason with him. "Even if, for the sake of argument, there had been another will, why would Lucas keep the original? He would destroy it the first chance he got.''

''No, he wouldn't,'' Bill insisted. ''He'd want to be able to gloat over it, thinking about how he'd outsmarted me and Dad. So you're going to help me find that will or I'll tell Lucas about us being lovers. And then where will your job be?''

Down the tubes, Jocelyn thought with horror. Just like her life. She stared blindly out the windshield at the wind-whipped snowflakes that had begun to fall.

''Think about it, babe. I'll be in touch.'' He gave her a self-satisfied smirk and got out of the car.

Numbly Jocelyn watched him swagger over to the silver Porsche parked behind her and get in.

What did she do now? she wondered frantically. She didn't have the slightest doubt that Bill would carry out his threat. Not only carry it out, but take a great deal of pleasure in doing it. There was a sadistic streak in the man a mile wide.

Which meant that she had to do something before he could act. But what? She closed her eyes and tried to think, not even noticing the bitter cold inside the car. Blind panic filled every cell of her consciousness. There was simply no room left for any other sensation.

''It isn't fair,'' she muttered as she started the car and pulled out of the parking lot, blinking back the tears that blurred her vision. But then, very little in her life to date had been fair, she thought tiredly.

# Chapter One

Jocelyn resisted the impulse to pull her thick winter coat more snugly around her, knowing that the chill she was feeling wasn't from the weather outside. It was coming from the silent man beside her.

Surreptitiously she studied Lucas Forester, her eyes lingering on the slight cleft in the middle of his square jaw. Longingly her gaze moved upward, searching for some hint of thawing in his formidable reserve, however slight. She couldn't find one. His lips were compressed, and his brown eyes were staring straight ahead. He could have been alone in the car for all the notice he was taking of her.

In just eight days she would have worked out her notice and she'd have to leave. Leave and never see him again. Panic filled her, but she refused to even acknowledge it. There was no point. One thing her miserable childhood had taught her, and taught her well, was never to rail against the Fates. It did no good. The Fates simply didn't give a damn. Either that or they had it in for her personally. And after this latest turn of events, she was beginning to wonder.

She chewed on her lip in impotent frustration. It was all so unfair. She hadn't done anything except to briefly think that Bill Forester might be someone special. It hadn't taken her very long to realize she was wrong. To figure out that he was an egomaniac who had exactly two interests in life. Himself and the pursuit of pleasure.

Lucas on he other hand... Instinctively her gaze returned to his beloved profile. Lucas's hard work had more than doubled the worth of his company in the five years since his father's death. And where he might take it in the next five years...

Pain lanced through her at the knowledge that she wouldn't be there to see him do it. At the thought of a future that didn't include daily contact with Lucas.

She'd get over it, she told herself, trying desperately to believe it and failing miserably. Lucas Forester made every man she had ever met fade into insignificance.

''I think I'll stop before we get to the airport for dinner,'' Lucas stated, and Jocelyn barely suppressed a shudder at his harsh tone. The indulgent, patient man she'd worked with for the past six months had vanished ten seconds after reading her resignation. If only it hadn't been necessary to give notice. If only she could have just not shown up for work. At least then she could have taken away happy memories of their last weeks together. Instead she would be left with the memories of a stranger. A rigidly polite, icily cold stranger who made no secret of the fact that he was furious at her sudden decision to quit. And for the flimsiest of reasons, as he'd pointed out to her when, in response to his demand to know why, she'd muttered something inane about needing time to find herself.

"Is that all right with you?" Lucas demanded, and Jocelyn jumped as the clipped sound of his voice sliced through her thoughts.

"Yes, that's fine," she hastily agreed.

"There's a place a few miles ahead that serves decent meals. Not that it would have to be much to be better than airline food," he said.

"No," Jocelyn answered cautiously, not sure if his comment called for an answer. Apparently it hadn't because he lapsed into silence again, concentrating on maneuvering over the icy patches the snowstorm had left on the road.

Stifling a sigh, Jocelyn resolutely focused on the dismal landscape outside the window. Buffalo in December looked as desolate as her heart felt.

Lucas shot a quick glance at the delicate lines of her averted profile and felt the now-familiar, stomach-churning mix of anger and betrayal flood him again. How could she even consider leaving him? For six months they had been a team. For six months they had worked closely together, laughing at the same things, feeling the same sense of outrage at the same societal ills, arguing amicably over the best way to fix those ills. He'd gone from thinking she was the best administrative assistant he'd ever had to believing that she was unique, a woman without a hidden agenda. A woman who could be trusted. He'd actually believed that she liked him, Lucas Forester the man, and not Lucas Forester the wealthy industrialist who could bankroll her every indulgence.

He'd gone from an abstract appreciation of her beauty to a realization that she was the most incredibly sensual woman he'd ever met. He'd spent long nights imagining all the ways he wanted to make love to her. He'd actually begun to believe that it could be safe to become emotionally involved with someone he employed. That business and pleasure could be successfully combined.

And with one short, typewritten page she'd shattered every one of his beliefs. In the length of time it had taken him to read her resignation, he'd realized that he'd been wrong. Dead wrong. None of the loyalty and liking she'd projected toward him were real. Not even the interest she'd shown in her job had been real.

Hell, she hadn't even bothered to lie about having found another position. She'd given him some song and dance about taking time off to find herself. What she'd undoubtedly found was some poor sucker who was willing to buy her what she wanted without the necessity of working for it.

Anger burned painfully in his chest. He was lucky, he told himself. Lucky to have found out that Jocelyn was just another fortune hunter before he had given her even an inkling that he...

Lucas instinctively shied away from examining exactly what he did feel for her, because it didn't make any difference. In eight more days she would be gone, and he'd never see her again. And he was glad, he told himself. His father's second marriage had taught him the absolute futility of loving a woman who wanted what a man owned and not what he was.

If only... He resolutely squashed the thought. Dwelling on might-have-beens was totally pointless.

A few miles further up the road, he caught sight of the restaurant he was looking for and, flipping on the turn signal, pulled into the lot. It took him a moment to find a place to park. It appeared that many other travelers were taking a break from the bad road conditions.

He pulled into one of the two last spaces and cut the engine. Getting out, he automatically rounded the car to open the door for Jocelyn, only to find that she had already scrambled out. Almost as if she were telling him that she wouldn't accept anything from him, he thought sourly. Not even an exhibition of good manners.

Frustrated, he shoved his hands into his pockets and stalked across the parking lot beside her. They were at the door before he realized that he'd forgotten his briefcase, which contained his cell phone. He needed to check in with Richard, his senior vice president, and find out what was going on back at the office.

"I forgot my cell phone." He bit out the words, and Jocelyn shuddered as their rough edges grated across her nerves. "Go inside. I'll be in as soon as I get it."

Without another word, Lucas turned on his heel and headed back toward the rented car.

Jocelyn watched his lean figure as he walked away from her, wanting to run after him to explain why she had to leave. But the impulse died instantly. It wouldn't work. She knew it wouldn't work. She'd been over and over her options in her mind a million times. After his father's disastrous second marriage to his secretary, Lucas was determined never to become emotionally involved with a woman who worked for him. When you added that bias to the fact that she had not only dated his hated half brother but had spent a night alone in a hotel room with him...

There was no way Lucas's casual liking for her would overcome both his own prejudices and the web of lies Bill would weave. Even if Lucas didn't fire her, he would view her with suspicion forever after. And she couldn't bear that.

Damn Bill! she thought savagely. How could he do this to her? Because he didn't think of her as a real person, she answered her own question. Bill moved through life as if he was the only real person in the world and everyone else was simply shadowy figures who had been put on earth to serve his needs.

Learn from the experience and go on. She repeated the mantra she had developed during a childhood spent in the uncertainties of foster care. But the thought brought no comfort. As far as she was concerned, after loving Lucas there was no place to go. No place but down. Down into a seemingly bottomless pit filled with pain and hopeless despair.

Maybe...

Jocelyn's absorption in her problems was broken by the black sedan that had suddenly appeared in the parking lot. It was going much too fast.

With a sudden spurt of speed the driver swung the car into the empty parking space next to Lucas, intent on beating out the minivan approaching the space from the opposite direction.

Jocelyn's breath caught in her throat as the sedan hit a patch of ice and began to skid sideways.

Sheer terror wrapped its clammy tentacles around Jocelyn's mind, freezing her in place. Horrified, she watched as the driver tried to regain control of his car and failed. The car continued its skid. There was an audible thump followed by the heart-rending sound of crunching metal as the sedan crashed into Lucas's car.

"No, please, God," Jocelyn whispered incoherently, straining to see Lucas over the bulk of the black sedan.

As if the sound of her voice were a key, she was suddenly released her from the paralyzing effects of her terror.

She sprinted across the parking lot intent on reaching Lucas. Her mind refused to even contemplate the idea that it might be too late to help him. The thought of a world that didn't contain the man she loved was too horrific to even contemplate.

She reached the sedan, and a quick glance showed her that Lucas was unconscious and trapped between his rental car and the sedan. Trapped and bleeding badly.

Racing around to the passenger side of the sedan, she pulled the door open. The middle-aged driver looked up and began to babble, "I didn't mean to hit him. It wasn't my fault! I slipped on the ice. It wasn't my fault, I tell you."

Furious that he was wasting time trying to justify his actions instead of helping Luke, Jocelyn grabbed the man's coat and, fueled by a surge of adrenaline that left her light-headed, yanked him out of the car.

"It'll be your fault if you don't get him help!" Jocelyn yelled at him as she shoved him backward. "Go call an ambulance."

"An ambulance?" the man parroted and then, when Jocelyn took a step toward him, hurriedly turned and starting running toward the restaurant.

Jocelyn slipped into the driver's seat of the man's car and turned the key in the ignition. To her profound relief, the engine turned over. Keeping her foot firmly on the brake so that the car didn't jump forward, she gently eased the car into Reverse. Once she was sure she was completely clear of Lucas, she hastily backed it completely out of the way and cut the engine.

Jumping out of the car, she ran back to Lucas who was lying on the pavement in a pool of blood.

She dropped to her knees beside him, trying to figure out where all the blood was coming from. His head, she quickly realized. She had to stop the bleeding, she thought as she watched the blood oozing from a wound that started on his right temple and ended somewhere in his thick brown hair.

Reaching into his inside suit pocket, she yanked out the pristine white handkerchief he always carried but never used.

The steady beat of his heart as her hand brushed across his broad chest steadied her somewhat. Maybe it wasn't as bad as it appeared, she tried to tell herself. Head wounds always looked worse than they really were because of all the blood. Anyone who watched television knew that.

Act now, worry later, she told herself, firmly pressing the cloth against the wound.

"Let me in there, miss. I'm a doctor." A strange man knelt beside her. His large, competent-looking hand closed over her makeshift bandage.

"Honey, get my bag out of the trunk." The man tossed the command over his shoulder.

An interminable moment later a plump, middle-aged woman carrying a black leather bag gently pushed Jocelyn out of the way and took her place.

"Don't you worry, dear," the woman told her. "My husband is as good as they come, and in my heyday I was one of the best O.R. nurses going."

"That's nice," Jocelyn muttered inanely, shivering convulsively as she retreated just far enough to give them room to work. If anything happened to Lucas, she didn't think she'd ever feel warm again.

Jocelyn closed her eyes and tried to pray, but she couldn't form a single coherent thought. The sight of Lucas's white, blood-stained face lying on the black tarmac filled her mind to the exclusion of everything.

"Good, the ambulance is here," she heard the doctor say, and Jocelyn turned around to see a green-and-white ambulance, its red lights flashing, pulling into the parking lot. Close on its heels was a black-and-white police cruiser.

"Unless I miss my guess, your husband is going to need surgery immediately," the doctor continued. "It's a good thing you're here to give permission. You are his wife, aren't you?" he asked, suddenly noticing her ringless fingers.

"Yes." Jocelyn had no compunction about lying. She'd do whatever it took to make sure Lucas got the help he needed.

"We work together, and I never wear my rings at the office." She tried to explain away her lack of a wedding ring.

She turned as the ambulance stopped and a husky man and a tall, thin woman jumped out. The man ran to Lucas, took one look and yelled something to the woman. She ran around the back of the ambulance, swung open the doors and yanked a large, red metal box out of it. Racing to Lucas, she squatted beside the doctor and her colleague.

"I tell you it wasn't my fault, Officer!" The sedan driver's whiny voice rasped across Jocelyn's ragged nerves.

She swung around and, her anger fueled by her stark fear for Lucas, snapped, "If you hadn't been going too fast, you wouldn't have skidded."

"What's the name of..." The policeman glanced down at Lucas's quiet form and winced.

"Lucas Forester," Jocelyn supplied.

"And this is his wife, Officer," the doctor said. "I'll be in the restaurant if you should need to talk to me.

"Try not to worry, my dear. We have an excellent local hospital." The doctor patted Jocelyn's shoulder and then turned and left.

Reaching into his pocket, the policeman pulled out a tissue and handed it to her.

"Wipe your face, Mrs. Forester. As cold as it is out here, your tears will freeze to your skin."

Tears? Jocelyn ran the back of her hand across her cheek, shocked to find it wet with tears. She scrubbed them away.

"I tell you it wasn't my fault. How was I supposed to know there was ice there?" the driver of the sedan insisted.

"Not only that, but when she yanked me out of my car, I think I sprained something," he complained.

The policeman studied Jocelyn's slight frame for a long moment before he turned and ran his eyes down the entire length of the man's well-padded, six-foot length.

"And why, sir, did the lady find it necessary to pull you out of your car?" the officer asked.

"I was shocked," the man blustered. "I was shocked and instead of letting me gather my wits, she just yanked open the door and pulled me out of my own car."

"Considering the amount of intelligence you had shown to date, waiting for you to find any wits you might have would have taken too long!" Jocelyn snapped.

"Well, I—"

"Go into the restaurant, sir, and wait there for me," the policeman ordered. "I'll be in to talk to you as soon as Mr. Forester is on his way to the hospital. Edna," the officer addressed his partner, "go along with him and make sure he doesn't have anything to drink. I don't want his blood alcohol results to be questioned."

"I have not been drinking!" The man glared at the policeman.

"Come along, sir," Edna took his arm in a firm grip and steered him toward the restaurant.

"Did you see the accident, Mrs. Forester?" the policeman asked Jocelyn.

"Yes, that man saw the last parking space, and he sped up to reach it before the van coming from the other direction got it. Lucas was getting something out of the car when the driver hit a patch of ice and slid into him."

"How did the car get off him?"

"I forced that—" Jocelyn glared at the departing back of the still volatile protesting man "—excuse for a driver out of his car, and I reversed it off Lucas."

"Excuse me." The husky emergency medical technician moved Jocelyn and the policeman aside so he could move in the stretcher.

Jocelyn watched intently as they loaded Lucas aboard the gurney.

"Don't you worry, ma'am." The technician paused long enough to give her a reassuring smile. "He's got a good, strong heartbeat, and head wounds always look much worse than they are. All that blood, you see."

Jocelyn stared at the gruesome stain on the parking tarmac and shuddered. She most certainly did see.

"How about if you ride to the hospital in the ambulance with your husband?" the technician said. "You can fill us in on his name and background as we go."

"You go along with your husband, Mrs. Forester," the policeman agreed. "Your car can't be driven now, anyway."

Jocelyn turned, briefly saw the extensive damage the sedan had done to the side of Lucas's rental car and dismissed it as unimportant. Nothing was important but Lucas.

She accepted the helping hand the policeman gave her into the ambulance and then huddled on a jump seat on one side, trying to stay out of the way of the paramedic who was taking Lucas's blood pressure.

"His pressure's holding well," the technician told Jocelyn. "Tell me, does he have any chronic conditions?"

"No," Jocelyn answered. "He jogs daily, so he's in good physical shape."

"Good," the man grunted as he started to rip open Lucas's white shirt.

Jocelyn bit back the urge to demand to know what he was doing. She didn't want to distract the man and thus endanger Lucas.

As she watched, he began to tape flat, disk-shaped things with wires attached to them to Lucas's chest.

"This is just a precaution," the technician said, rewarding Jocelyn's patience with information. "The hospital is getting the readout now and they'll be able to respond the minute we get him there."

"How much longer?" Jocelyn shivered at the sight of Lucas's white face. The very faint shadow of his emerging beard showed up starkly against the abnormal pallor of his cheeks, giving him a slightly raffish look. The look was reinforced by the nasty bruise beginning to emerge on the left side of his face.

"We'll be there soon." The man braced himself against the side of the ambulance as the driver swung around a curve.

Five minutes later they pulled up in front of the emergency room door of the hospital, and a team of white-coated personnel erupted through the doors and swarmed into the ambulance. To her relief, the people seemed to know exactly what they were doing. Within seconds they had Lucas out of the ambulance and were rushing him through the double doors.

"Come on, Mrs. Forester," the technician said. "I'll show you where you can wait."

"Thank—" Her voice broke under the force of the emotions she was trying to hold in check.

"Try not to think about it." The man took her arm and steered her into the emergency waiting room.

Not thinking about Lucas was like trying not to breathe. It only worked until your instincts took over, and then you automatically started again.

"You can wait in here, Mrs. Forester." The man showed her into a small waiting room furnished with a black vinyl couch and an orange plastic chair. "You sit down, and I'll go tell the doctor where you are, all right?"

Jocelyn nodded jerkily and sank onto the couch. She clenched her hands into fists and stared down at them, shocked when she saw a tear fall and bounce off her white knuckles. Impatiently she wiped her cheeks with her coat sleeve and then started to pick up her purse to get a tissue. Her purse wasn't there. Vaguely she glanced around the room, wondering where it was and then dismissed its whereabouts as unimportant. There was nothing in her purse that couldn't be replaced, whereas Lucas...

Jocelyn swallowed the raw taste of fear.

"Mrs. Forester, I'm so glad you're here." A tall, elderly man bustled into the room. "I'm Dr. Edwards, the staff neurosurgeon, and I've just seen your husband. We're doing an MRI at the moment, and as soon as that is done I want to go in."

"In?" Jocelyn repeated blankly.

"Operate," the man said succinctly. "There's intercranial bleeding going on and it has to be stopped.

"It's extremely fortunate you were with him or we would have lost precious time trying to locate the next of kin."

Jocelyn shuddered. She wasn't sure whether his half brother or his stepmother would be considered his next of kin, but one thing she did know, neither one of them would have lifted a finger to help him. They valued Lucas's possessions, not Lucas himself. In fact, she thought, as she remembered Bill's hard eyes glaring at her, she wouldn't put it past Bill to stall giving his consent in the hope that Lucas might suffer permanent brain damage. Her stomach lurched. Or worse.

She didn't dare let the doctor find out she wasn't Lucas's wife. Not until after he was out of danger. Then she'd confess.

Taking a deep breath, Jocelyn said, "I'll sign whatever is necessary to ensure...my husband's recovery." The word husband rang mockingly in her ears. For so long she'd dreamed of Lucas coming to love her, and now that there was no chance of that ever happening, she was publicly claiming him as her husband.

Her breath caught on a sob at the irony of it.

"I know it's hard, Mrs. Forester, but try not to worry. The MRI was looking good when I left. With just the smallest amount of luck, he'll sail through the operation and by Christmas, all he'll have to remember this by is a scar, which any good plastic surgeon can take care of.

"Now, you try and relax, and I'll send the secretary in with the release forms for you to sign. I'm going to go prep him for surgery."

Jocelyn nodded, not trusting herself to speak without breaking down in tears.

Jocelyn watched the doctor leave and then stared down at her tightly clenched hands and tried to think, to plan her next step. She couldn't. Her thoughts kept getting sucked down into the maelstrom of emotions swirling through her. Finally she just gave up and stared blankly at the beige wall. All she could do was to endure and wait for the operation to be over.

Despite the kindness of the workers in the emergency room, who kept bringing her cups of coffee and offering hearty words of encouragement that rang false to Jocelyn's ears, the wait seemed interminable.

Finally, when Jocelyn had about reached the end of her tether, the doctor strode through the doorway. His wide grin told her everything she wanted to know.

Relief washed over her in waves. A high-pitched buzzing filled her ears. Jocelyn shook her head to try to clear the sound, and the movement snapped her link with consciousness. A dark gray fog closed over her, carrying her into a blissful silence.

She came to a few minutes later to find herself lying on the sofa she had been sitting on, a worried-looking doctor bending over her. For a fraction of a second she was confused, and then she remembered.

"He's okay?" she demanded.

"Completely out of danger. I stopped the bleeding, and as far as I can tell there was no damage."

"As far as you can tell?" Jocelyn repeated. "What does that mean?"

"Exactly what it says. I saw nothing to indicate that he will have any lasting effects of his accident. I've spoken to the social worker here at the hospital. She's checked you into one of the rooms we keep available for the relatives of patients in intensive care. And the policeman brought your suitcases from your wrecked car and your purse, which you apparently left behind. They've been put in the room."

"Thank you, when can I see my…husband?" the word sounded odd on her lips. Odd and yet strangely right.

"He's in recovery at the moment. He should be out in

an hour if he continues to make such good progress. Why don't you go to your room and lie down. I promise I'll get you the minute we move him down to the ward. Okay?''

''Okay,'' Jocelyn said, willing to agree to anything which would allow her to see her beloved Lucas.

# *Chapter Two*

"Doctor Edwards asked that you see him before you visited your husband this morning," the nurse told Jocelyn when she reached the nurses' station of the surgical ward.

Jocelyn felt her skin blanch with sudden fear. What had happened? Even though Lucas hadn't yet regained consciousness, the nurses had been very pleased with his vital signs when she'd left him late last night.

"Lucas didn't..." Jocelyn couldn't bring herself to complete the sentence.

"No, of course not," the nurse hurriedly reassured her. "He's coming along nicely. Amazingly well, in fact, considering what he's been through. It's just that...

"Oh, good, there's Dr. Edwards now." The nurse broke off in evident relief as she caught sight of the doctor hurrying down the hall toward them.

Jocelyn turned, waiting nervously for the doctor to reach her. If Lucas hadn't suffered a relapse, the only reason she could think of that the doctor would insist on seeing her would be if the hospital had somehow found out that Lucas and she weren't married. That she had lied to them.

Which would explain the doctor's impatience to see her. He was probably worried about the hospital's liability for having operated on Lucas without proper authorization.

Jocelyn braced her thin shoulders and prepared to face the doctor's wrath. But even knowing that what she'd done was technically wrong, she'd do it again in a heartbeat. Lucas had gotten the help he'd needed when he'd needed it. Not when some bureaucrat had decided it was legally safe to treat him.

"Mrs. Forester." Dr. Edwards's greeting caught her off guard. If he'd found out that she wasn't Lucas's wife, why was he still calling her that? And if he hadn't found out, then why was it so urgent he speak to her? Unless the nurse had lied about Lucas being okay? Sudden panic gripped her, and she took an involuntary step toward the doctor.

"Lucas is fine." The doctor had no trouble reading her expressive face. "Physically, I'm very impressed with how well he's responding."

"But?" Jocelyn asked, sensing his constraint.

"It has been my experience that occasionally in situations like this—"

"Cut to the chase," Jocelyn said, interrupting him. "My nerves won't last through the buildup."

"Don't worry. It's nothing bad. Just a temporary problem. Mr. Forester is suffering a spot of amnesia."

"Amnesia?" Jocelyn stared blankly at the doctor.

"It isn't all that uncommon in head injuries," he assured her. "We discovered it this morning when we cut back on the pain medication enough to let him regain consciousness. Your husband should remember everything within a week. A couple of weeks at the outside."

"Amnesia," Jocelyn repeated. "As in, he doesn't remember who I am?" Or the fact that I'm not really his wife? A complicated mixture of emotions swirled through her as the implications of the situation began to register.

"Not at the moment," he said.

"How do I handle this?" she finally asked.

"The most important thing you can do is to keep calm and not to try to force his memory. He should remember a little more each day until it all comes back to him. Just answer any questions he asks and, above all, keep stress to a minimum."

"I see," Jocelyn said slowly, wondering what to do now. Confessing who she really was was out of the question in light of this latest development. Not if Lucas was to have the peace he needed to get better. At the first hint of any weakness on Lucas's part, Bill would be all over him; and Bill was stress personified.

Besides, she didn't really want to confess, she realized. Soon she would be gone from Lucas's life entirely. Being able to pretend to be his wife for a few days was a gift of incredible proportions from an unexpectedly benevolent fate. She'd be able to cherish the memory of those precious days for the rest of her life.

"When can he leave the hospital?" she asked.

"Barring anything unforeseen, he can be discharged day after tomorrow."

"So soon!"

"He'll recover much quicker in a familiar environment. Don't worry. You'll be fine." Dr. Edwards gave her an encouraging smile and hurried off down the hall.

I sure hope he's a better doctor than he is a fortune teller, Jocelyn thought. Because "fine" was the one thing she wasn't going to be. Once Lucas regained his memory, she'd lose the man she loved. She didn't think she'd ever be fine again. Which was all the more reason to make the most of the moment, she told herself.

Taking a deep breath, she hurried down the hall to Lucas's room. Pushing open the door, she walked inside.

Lucas lay in a high, narrow bed. His eyes were closed, and his skin had a grayish cast, which was emphasized by the large, white bandage, which covered the left side of his forehead. Jocelyn silently approached the bed, wincing when she saw the lurid purple-and-red bruise that started under his bandage and ran down his cheek almost to his jaw. He hadn't shaved since the accident, and the three days' growth of beard gave him a vaguely pirate-like look that sent an unexpected kick of excitement through her. Lucas looked like an ancient warrior. One who'd been on the losing side.

Her heart twisted. He looked so vulnerable. Something that was totally foreign to his normal vibrant personality. Lucas always seemed so competent, so absolutely in charge of both himself and the situation he found himself in; it was a shock to realize that he needed protecting. But she also found it oddly exhilarating. Somehow, his present vulnerability put them on an equal footing. He needed her. For the first time in their relationship she wasn't on the periphery of his life. She was smack in the middle of it.

His eyelids slowly lifted as if he'd sensed someone was in the room with him, and she found herself staring into his eyes. They seemed dimmer than usual. The brilliant sparkle that usually lit them had been dulled, which was hardly surprising given what had happened, she told herself.

Uncertainly she watched him, waiting for a clue as to how to proceed.

Lucas squinted, trying to see the woman standing beside his bed through the haze of pain that engulfed him. Her large eyes were pale blue with an intriguing violet tinge, he thought distractedly. But her eyes didn't look hopeful. They were filled with apprehension. Because of him? he wondered as he studied the creamy texture of her complexion. Her delicately molded nose had a light dusting of pale freckles that intrigued him. Did she have freckles anywhere else? he wondered. His eyes instinctively dropped to her body and a surge of heat welled up through him, which increased the pounding in his head to nauseating levels.

Hastily, he forced his gaze upward away from the temptation of her body to discover her mouth. She had gorgeous lips, he decided after a moment's deliberation. They were soft and pink and full and promised unimaginable delights to anyone lucky enough to kiss them.

Mesmerized, he watched as she reached up and brushed back a strand of her gleaming hair. It was the exact color of Italian chestnuts. A deep rich brown with just the slightest hint of red in the mix.

Who was she? he wondered. Certainly not a nurse. Not dressed in that severely cut, dark-blue business suit. He wished he could see her legs over the edge of the bed. If they were as intriguing as her face was…

A sudden flash of memory of her reaching up to get something on a shelf over her head flashed through his mind. She was wearing beige slacks that lovingly molded her trim hips. The instinctive burst of desire that surged through him made the pain in his head escalate to appalling proportions. He waited a moment for the pain to ebb before he followed his memory flash to its logical conclusion. He knew this woman. He knew her from before the accident. Knew her and desired her. Hell, he thought with black humor, if he desired her much more he'd pass out from the pain it caused him.

His eyes narrowed thoughtfully. This morning when he'd tried to ask the doctor some questions, the only information that the man had actually given him had been that Lucas had a wife named Jocelyn, and she had been in the hospital since the accident, although she wasn't there at the moment. Could this woman be his wife? He tried to slow his breathing to counter his sudden excitement at the tantalizing thought. His eyes dropped to her breasts. Did he know her intimately? Frustration engulfed him at his inability to remember.

Sending up a prayer that this intriguing-looking woman really belonged to him, he gave her a crooked grin and said, "Mrs. Forester, I presume?"

To his dismay her lovely blue eyes suddenly filled with tears.

"Oh, Lucas, I was so worried that..." Her musical voice broke, drowned in the depth of her relief. Lucas sounded so normal. So lucid. So...so Lucas.

"That I'd forgotten you?" he said, drawing his own conclusions. "Come closer. I don't bite. In fact," he added when she didn't move, "even thinking lascivious thoughts at the moment makes my head pound, quite literally."

He frowned as a deep flush burned beneath her pale skin.

"You are my wife, aren't you?" he asked uncertainly, confused at her odd reaction. Didn't wives want their husbands to desire them? Or was it that this particular wife didn't want him to desire her? Or was her seemingly embarrassed reaction caused by something else entirely? He winced as his head began to pound with his conjectures.

Jocelyn took a deep breath and said, "Yes, I'm your wife."

Her words seemed to bounce off the room's bare walls, gaining strength as they ricocheted. Jocelyn listened to them, both elated and scared by what she had done. One of the many foster mothers she'd had when she was a child had once told her that, if she told a lie, God would strike her dead on the spot.

All her life she'd felt a nervous dread whenever she told a fib, even though she knew perfectly well that God had better things to do than to run around zapping people. But this certainly proved her foster mother had been wrong once and for all, Jocelyn thought ruefully. Because if instantaneous retribution hadn't been demanded for a lie of this magnitude, she was safe forever.

"I knew you were familiar," Lucas said, giving up trying to analyze the expressions flitting across her expressive face. She was probably just upset, which was hardly surprising. His accident hadn't done anything for his mental health, either.

Instinctively he reached out to her as his head began to pound again.

Jocelyn grasped his hand. Unable to resist the temptation, she stroked her fingertips across the back of his hand, savoring the texture of his warm skin. A spurt of excitement shafted through her as he began to lightly rub his thumb over the palm of her hand in response to her caress. Her breathing shortened as a shivery sensation raced over her nerve endings.

Jocelyn ran the tip of her tongue over her suddenly dry lips.

Lucas watched the movement of her tongue from beneath his lowered eyelids, wanting to trace its path with his own tongue. And then he wanted to…

"Just a minute while I get a chair to sit in." Jocelyn's voice came out in a breathless squeak. Tugging her hand free, she hurried across the room to get the black vinyl armchair against the other wall.

Lucas watched as she dragged it across the floor, his sense of unease increasing. Did she really want the chair or did she just want to break off the physical contact with him? He clenched his teeth together in frustration at his inability to remember and immediately paid a price when his head started to pound again. Deliberately he tried to relax. This wasn't the time to go paranoid, he tried to tell himself. He had enough on his plate trying to deal with the aftereffects of his accident. He didn't need to be imagining problems where there might not be any.

Unless... Another more ominous possibility occurred to him and his eyes shot open. Could she know something about his operation that he didn't? Could the doctor have told her he wasn't ever going to remember again? That his life to date was now dead to him? Fear shafted through him, sending a sheen of sweat over his skin.

"Lucas, what's wrong?" Jocelyn caught his sudden spurt of emotion and feared that he might have remembered everything.

"What did that doctor tell you?" he demanded.

"Tell me?" she repeated, torn between relief that he hadn't regained his memory yet and guilt at being so selfish as to be glad.

"About my operation?"

"That you were very lucky. That there would be no permanent damage and that memory loss wasn't unusual after this kind of operation and that all we had to do was wait for it to come back."

"That's it? Just wait?"

"All those cartoons where they wap amnesia victims

over the head to give them back their memory are just that, cartoons. Although…'' She studied his annoyed features speculatively. ''If you turn out to be a bad patient, I might be tempted to try it.''

Lucas heard the laughter threading her voice and instinctively relaxed.

''That's what he told me, too,'' he confessed. ''At least, the bit about just waiting. But what am I supposed to do in the meantime? Vegetate?''

Jocelyn flushed as a flood of activities that had nothing to do with vegetation poured through her mind. Not now, she ordered herself. Now she needed to reassure Lucas that everything would be normal. Later she could indulge in daydreams.

''At the moment your job is to lie there and rest,'' she told him.

''What a boring scenario,'' he grumbled. ''Now, if you were offering to share the bed with me…''

''You're supposed to be avoiding undue excitement.'' Jocelyn struggled to sound more sophisticated than she felt.

''In that case, how about some background?'' Lucas changed the subject. ''Tell me what happened to land me here. All that doctor would say is I had an accident and not to worry about it.''

''He doesn't want you subjected to any stress,'' Jocelyn explained.

''He doesn't think not knowing isn't stressful?''

''There really isn't all that much to know,'' Jocelyn said, happy to talk about something that didn't involve her lying to him.

''We were on our way back to the airport—''

''Back? We don't live here? And where is here, for that matter?''

''Here is Buffalo, New York. You were here to finalize your buying Bleffords Plastics.''

''And you came along for the ride?''

''I came along because I happen to be your highly qualified administrative assistant,'' Jocelyn shot back. She might love Lucas to distraction, but she had no intention of playing the helpless little woman. Even if she was a little rattled at the moment by the whole course of events.

''Really?'' His right eyebrow disappeared into his bandage as his surprise showed. ''You seem much too decorative to be a highly efficient anything.''

''And you seem much too smart to be succumbing to stereotypes! I'm beginning to think that you got hit harder than I thought.''

Lucas grinned at her, fascinated at the way her indignation made her eyes sparkle. ''Maybe I'm secretly a closet chauvinist, and having lost my memory I don't know that I have to pretend.''

''Keep that up and you'll lose more than your memory—you'll lose your head. I am a competent professional, and I demand respect for my business skills.''

''What about your skills as a wife?'' Lucas slipped the question in.

What was going on? Jocelyn wondered uneasily. Why was Lucas's every sentence suddenly imbued with sexual meaning? They'd worked together for more than six months and their sexual interaction had been virtually nil. Now all of a sudden his every comment was a double entendre.

But then, she'd never claimed to be his wife before. Apparently this was the way he responded to a wife. On the other hand, the way he normally treated her, as a sexless but valued colleague, was the way he responded to a female employee. There was no doubt about it, she decided. Being treated as a wife was a whole lot more fun.

"I'm long-suffering," she said repressively.

Lucas grinned at her. "Really? Tell me more."

"I'm not supposed to try to force your memory," Jocelyn said, not wanting to tell too many outright lies.

"Okay." Lucas suddenly switched into what Jocelyn recognized as his work mode. "So we were in Buffalo on business and then what happened?"

"You decided to stop at a restaurant for dinner on our way to the airport. We were almost to the door of the restaurant when you realized you'd left your cell phone in the car. You went back for it. A driver pulled into the space beside you and skidded on the ice. He pinned you between the cars." Her voice thinned with remembered terror.

To his intense frustration, her recounting of the accident meant nothing to him. She could have been telling him something that had happened to a complete stranger. Nor did he want to keep pushing her for details, because talking about the accident was clearly upsetting her.

Not only that but his pounding head was making rational thought difficult. And the drugs they'd insisted on giving him tended to make the world distinctly fuzzy around the edges.

"I love you." He tentatively tried out the words and found to his relief that they sounded exactly right. "I love you, Jocelyn Forester. I love you, Mrs. Lucas Forester." His voice gained strength as he tried out different variants of her name. Whether he could remember her or not, he was sure he loved her. Nothing that felt so right to say could be a lie.

Jocelyn swallowed, feeling suffocated by guilt. When events had propelled her into her impersonation, she hadn't thought about how Lucas would react to being told he was married to her.

"It's your turn," Lucas said watching her intently.

She'd just have to live with her guilt, she told herself. She couldn't back out now. Lucas needed her. Needed her to give him enough space to heal. It was the only personal thing she would ever be able to do for him, and she had no intention of failing him.

"I...I love you, Lucas," she blurted out.

"What do I do?" To her intense relief, he changed the subject.

"You are the sole owner of a medium-size company that makes component parts for lots of things. You inherited the company when your father died five years ago and have since doubled it in size," she answered promptly.

"Do I have any other family?" Lucas asked.

"Your mother has been dead since you were four, and your father remarried not long after. You have a stepmother and a half brother."

She studied Lucas narrowly, trying to see if the mention of Bill had caused him to remember anything.

He sighed, having no trouble interpreting her look. "Sorry, I don't remember a thing about either my family or any kind of widget. Do I like doing whatever it is I do?"

"Yes," Jocelyn said honestly. "You were determined to be the biggest and best of your kind."

Had his concentration on work taken its toll on his marriage? he suddenly wondered. Was that what was causing the odd vibes he kept picking up from her whenever the conversation got personal?

Yet another question he didn't have an answer for. But this was hardly the time to move any personal problems they might have to center stage. Not when he couldn't remember them. Far better to leave them buried for the time being, he decided.

"So who's running the company while I'm lying here?" he asked. "You?"

"Not me." She gave him a rueful smile. "I've been pacing up and down the hall outside while the doctor rearranged the inside of your head to his liking."

Lucas grimaced. "It feels like he's still in there."

Jocelyn eyed him uncertainly. Was he paler now than when she'd arrived? She wasn't sure. But she was sure that the lines beside his mouth were deeper.

"Do you need something for the pain?"

"No! No," he moderated his voice as her eyes widened. "I don't want any more of their drugs."

Jocelyn shrugged. "It's your head and your choice. I just want you to get better."

"If you aren't minding the store, then who is?" he asked, returning to the subject of his business.

"Richard has agreed to look after things until you're well."

An elderly face with a thatch of white hair and a neatly trimmed white beard flashed through his mind, followed by a feeling of intense relief. The doctor hadn't been lying. He was going to regain his memory. It was all there. It was just a matter of giving his memories time to work their way to the surface.

"I've been thinking about where you can recuperate in peace," she said slowly. It was a problem to which she'd given a great deal of thought. It had to be somewhere where they wouldn't run into anyone who knew either of them and would know they weren't married, and it also had to be someplace away from Bill. Because if Bill were to find out that Lucas had lost his memory...

"And did you reach any conclusions?" Lucas asked.

"Yes, your ski lodge seems our best bet."

He frowned slightly as he tried to pull an image out of his mind and failed.

"Where is it?" he asked

"In Vermont, near Stowe. A great-uncle on your mother's side of the family gave it to you when you graduated from college," she added at his blank look.

"Since the doctor is very emphatic about not wanting you to get overtired, I thought we'd just fly directly to Vermont from the hospital. We can buy any clothes we need up there."

"All right," Lucas agreed. He didn't really care where they went as long as she was with him.

## *Chapter Three*

"How do you feel?" Jocelyn took her eyes off the empty road leading to Lucas's ski lodge to give him a quick sideways glance, her gaze lingering for a fraction of a second on the scar which started at his temple and ended in his thick hair. It was a bright red at the moment, but the surgeon had assured her it would fade in time.

Lucas's cheeks appeared slightly leaner than they had been before the accident. As if he'd lost weight during his stay in the hospital. And the lines around the corners of his eyes were more deeply scored. As if the pain he'd endured had widened his normal laugh lines.

"I'm fine," Lucas said.

"Does your head hurt?" she persisted.

"Nothing an aspirin can't handle."

"I hardly think aspirin will work," Jocelyn said.

"Don't fuss, woman," Lucas said. "Haven't you heard that aspirin is a wonder drug?"

"The wonder is that you've come out of this in one piece."

She shuddered as the memory of his crumpled body lying on the pavement flashed through her mind.

"Except for the minor fact that I can't remember anything," he said dryly.

"Your memory will come back." The surgeon had assured them of it when he'd released Lucas from the hospital that morning.

"It'd better be soon. You're sure my vice president is competent to run my company?"

"Positive, and like I told you, Christmas is a slack time at work. Everyone has other things on their minds."

Including me, she thought. Especially me. Jocelyn took a deep breath to try to control the emotions churning through her. Ever since they'd left the hospital, she'd felt as if she'd wandered into that old television show called *Fantasy Island.* It was as if some powerful wizard had arranged to give her a taste of what she wanted more than anything else in the world. To be Lucas's wife. But that same wizard had included a nasty wild card in the mix—the knowledge that Lucas might regain his memory at any minute and turn her dream into a nightmare.

Jocelyn nervously chewed on her lower lip as she contemplated Lucas's reaction to her deception. She could probably make him understand why she'd pretended to be his wife in the first place. Making sure that he received the proper medical attention as soon as possible made sense and could be easily defended. Where it was going to get tricky would be trying to explain why she had continued her impersonation once he was out of danger. Maybe she could tell him that she had been afraid the hospital would contact his half brother to provide care, and she had been worried about what Bill might do?

It had the distinct advantage of being the truth, just not all the truth. But Lucas might not realize that.

But whether he believed her or not, she had to stop worrying about the future or she wouldn't be able to enjoy the present.

She'd never spent Christmas with someone she loved before, and she was determined to savor this one as long as and as hard as she could.

"Why so serious?" Lucas studied the deserted country road in front of them. "Are you tired after the flight? I can drive for a while. I must know how."

Jocelyn gave a gurgle of laughter.

She had the most enchanting laugh, he thought. It made him feel warm and happy. As if something wonderful were about to happen.

"Thanks, anyway, but I'll drive. Finding out how much you remember about driving is not something I want to try on a snowy mountain road."

"I guess not," Lucas muttered absently as an image of skiing over the snow briefly flashed through his mind. He could almost feel the icy snow hitting his face and the warmth of the afternoon sun on his back.

"Did you remember something?" Jocelyn noticed his abstracted expression and felt a sudden flash of fear.

Lucas caught the tension in her voice. Clearly his loss of memory bothered her a great deal. Which was hardly surprising, he conceded. Being married to someone who didn't remember you must be stressful in the extreme. It was no wonder she seemed on edge every time his amnesia was mentioned. It would probably be easier on her nerves if he didn't mention his disconcerting flashes of memory.

"No, but I'm working on it." He made his voice purposefully cheerful. "Did we spend last Christmas at this ski lodge we're going to?"

Jocelyn briefly weighed lying and saying yes, but then

decided that the fewer lies she told, the fewer lies she'd have to remember. And apologize for later.

"We weren't married last Christmas."

"When did we get married?"

Wildly Jocelyn searched her memory, trying to come up with a date that would be easy to remember. Halloween, she decided. This whole affair had a distinct flavor of trick or treat to it.

"October thirty-first," she said.

"And what kind of wedding was it? Formal?" He waited hopefully for a flash of memory. For an image, however brief, of Jocelyn in a long, white, flowing dress, her face hidden by a white veil, walking down the aisle toward him. To his disappointment his mind remained a blank.

"No. We just got a license and were married by a justice of the peace," she said shortly. "Are you sure your head isn't bothering you? Maybe you ought to try to rest a minute."

And quit asking her questions that she didn't want to answer, Lucas drew the obvious conclusion. But why didn't she want to talk about their wedding? Unless she resented the fact that they had gotten married in what sounded like a hole-in-the-corner affair? But if she had disliked being married by a justice of the peace, why had she agreed to it? A woman as gorgeous and intelligent as Jocelyn was could have her pick of husbands. And she'd picked him. The sense of pride and satisfaction that filled him was quickly followed by a rush of doubt. Why had she picked him?

Drop it, Forester, he told himself. You're only going to upset her by pushing.

"Maybe a rest is a good idea," Lucas said, leaning his

head back against the seat and closing his eyes to shut out the glare from the bright afternoon sun.

To his surprise he drifted into a light sleep that lasted until Jocelyn turned sharply, and the deeply rutted driveway proved a challenge to the suspension system of the Mercedes they'd rented at the airport.

Lucas opened his eyes and looked around curiously. In front of them was a small, one-story house covered in grayed cedar shakes. It seemed to have grown out of the hillside. But despite the bleak color, the house seemed to exude a welcoming air. As if it had been patiently waiting for him to return, he thought fancifully, and then blinked as he got a flash of a crackling fire blazing merrily in a fieldstone fireplace.

"Recognize it?" Jocelyn asked.

"No, but it seems very welcoming. Did we spend much time here?"

"I've never been here, but you used to spend every free weekend you had up here."

"Don't you like the country?" Lucas asked as he got out of the car.

Jocelyn looked around, her eyes lingering on a plump chickadee sitting on a tree stump in front of the house. As she watched, the cheerful little bird ruffled its feathers and flew away.

"I don't know. I've never been out of the city on more than a day trip."

Lucas reached past her into the car trunk and pulled out their two suitcases.

"Let me take those," she said when Lucas started toward the house with both suitcases.

"I hurt my head, not my back," he said.

Jocelyn hurried after him, swallowing her protests. It probably wouldn't hurt him, she told herself. The doctor had been emphatic about only one thing. Lucas was to do nothing that might cause him to suffer another blow to the head.

"Open it, would you?" Lucas paused in front of the door.

"I don't have a key," she said.

Why didn't she have a key? he wondered. Even if she hadn't been here before, why wouldn't he have given his wife a key to a property he owned? For that matter, why wouldn't she have demanded one? Maybe they just hadn't gotten around to it yet. He tried to stifle his sense of unease. After all, they'd been married less than two months.

Setting down the suitcases, he reached into his pocket, pulled out his key ring and stared at it. This time he was met with no answering flash of memory.

"Um, would you happen to know which one is the door key? Or even if it's on this ring?" he asked.

"If?" Jocelyn's voice rose. "I never thought to ask you if you had a key. I just assumed..."

Her voice trailed away as she stared thoughtfully at the window to the side of the door. It looked pretty burglar-proof to her. She shivered as an icy gust of wind slithered down her neck.

Lucas chuckled. "Asking me wouldn't have done much good. We'll simply have to try them all."

"You try, and I'll pray like mad that we don't freeze to death before we find a way in." She shivered again.

"It isn't cold enough out here to freeze," Lucas said with a cheerfulness Jocelyn felt was totally unfounded.

"Try telling that to my body, which is slowly going numb."

"That I can fix." He shot her a wicked look that sped up her heart rate. "I'll just...

"Ah, success!" The door swung open with the second

key he tried. With a courtly gesture, he motioned her into the house.

Curious, Jocelyn crossed the threshold and looked around. They were standing in a large room. On the wall to their left was a floor-to-ceiling fieldstone fireplace with a raised hearth. To one side of it was a brown leather sofa and across from it were two leather chairs that shared an ottoman. The wall directly opposite the door had a double set of sliding glass doors that led out onto a wooden deck. In the wall to her right were two doors. One was closed, but the other was open and she could see a small kitchen.

''Nice,'' Lucas murmured as the peaceful feeling of the house began to seep into him.

''Very,'' Jocelyn agreed. ''In fact, with a little color splashed around it would be downright cheerful.''

Jocelyn took a quick look at Lucas's drawn features and said, ''Let's find the bed.''

''Now, that's an idea I can relate to,'' he said. ''Bed sounds positively invigorating.''

Alerted by an odd note in his voice, Jocelyn looked at him and found his eyes gleaming with emotion. Her mouth suddenly dried as his gaze slipped down the length of her body. She shivered, feeling his gaze as if it were an actual touch. Surely he didn't think she had meant…

''You need to rest,'' she blurted out.

''You rest your way and I'll rest mine, and I'll guarantee you mine's more fun.'' His sensual smile hit her with the force of a blow. She wasn't sure how she would classify making love to Lucas, but fun seemed to be massively understating the case. Earthshaking seemed a little closer.

Jocelyn swallowed as she scrambled to pull her scattered thoughts together. Now what? She flogged her tired mind. The man thought they were married. And he thought that because she'd told him so. Much as she wanted to make love to him, she couldn't. Tricking him into making love with her would degrade everything she felt for him. It would turn something that should be wonderful into something furtive and sordid. Not only that but she would never, ever, be able to come up with a logical explanation for going to bed with him. He'd be left to conclude that she was either so madly in love with him that she was willing to grab any chance she got to make love with him or that she was so lacking in values that she was willing to sleep with a man she didn't have a relationship with. Both explanations were unacceptable.

"I'm hardly likely to hurt myself making love to you," Lucas said, disquieted by her obvious reluctance.

"The doctor said that we weren't supposed to make love for a month or so." Jocelyn eagerly grasped at the excuse that his words had suggested to her.

"A month!" Lucas repeated incredulously. "We're married."

"And we'll have the rest of our lives together." Jocelyn forced the lie out. "What's a month?"

"Do you really want to know?" he asked dryly.

"Just have patience," Jocelyn urged. "A month will pass before you know it."

"It would appear that I don't have any choice," he grumbled.

"Why don't you go lie down and rest and I'll—"

"I just had a nap. Why don't I build a fire instead."

"A fire would be nice," she agreed. "Actually any kind of heat would be nice." She shivered as the room's chill began to seep into her bones.

"There has to be some kind of central heating system." Lucas frowned as he noticed her shivers. She must be tired after coping with all the details of checking him out of the hospital and then the plane trip from Buffalo to Vermont followed by the drive to the lodge from the airport. He certainly didn't want her coming down with anything. Other than himself.

He turned and scanned the walls, quickly finding what appeared to be a thermostat. Walking over to it, he flipped it up from the fifty it was set on to seventy-two. To his relief, there was an instant rumbling sound and warm air began to pour out of the register to his right.

"Ask and ye shall receive," he announced.

If only it were that easy, Jocelyn thought, suppressing a sigh. There was so much she would like to have, and all of it centered on the man standing in front of her. But at least she was going to have a few days with him. Maybe even a couple of weeks, if the doctor was accurate in his estimated time for Lucas to regain his memory.

"Now for a fire," he said, looking around him as if he expected to find a lit match lying in the middle of the room.

"How does one start a fire?" Jocelyn asked.

"You're asking me, when I can't remember my own name?" he said dryly. "But it stands to reason that I must have used that fireplace and, if I did, it also makes sense that I would know how to start a fire."

"Sounds logical," Jocelyn agreed. "How do we test the theory?"

"I'll go outside and see if I can find a woodpile to raid. You look for something to use as a starter."

Jocelyn bit back the impulse to say she'd get the wood. If she hung over him and tried to restrict his movements beyond those the doctor had outlined, she would be bound to annoy him.

Jocelyn watched as he went outside through the sliding glass doors. The sooner she got them some clothes more suitable to a ski lodge, the better. His cashmere dress coat was not meant for hauling wood.

Jocelyn opened the closed door beside the kitchen to find herself in a small bedroom dominated by a king-size bed. A triple dresser stood against one wall, and to her right an open door led into what appeared to be the house's only bathroom.

The bedroom had a deserted look as if Lucas hadn't been here for a long time. And he probably hadn't, she realized. They'd both worked every Saturday since July, and this place was too far to come for just one day.

Since nothing in the room looked as if it might serve to start a fire, she headed to the house's only other room, the kitchen. Relatively small, it had appliances and cabinets along two sides with a small table in the alcove next to an outside door that led to the deck.

Compact, but functional. Jocelyn approved. She opened the cabinet door under the sink and discovered a plastic container with a stack of old newspapers in it.

Thoughtfully she pulled the top sheet out and read the date. April seventh. She'd been right. Lucas hadn't been here since last spring. She pulled the container out and carried it back into the living room where she found Lucas in the process of dumping an armful of logs on the hearth.

Jocelyn winced at the dirt and leaves that clung to the front of his coat.

"What'd you find?" Lucas absently brushed the debris off, scattering it onto the beige carpet.

Jocelyn resolutely ignored it. It was his house, and if leaves and twigs on the carpet didn't bother him, she wouldn't let it bother her.

"Newspaper." She held out the container. "If we crumple it up, it should work okay. Shouldn't it?" she added as he continued to stare at the paper.

"I suppose," he said slowly, "but I don't think that's what I normally do."

"Why do you think that?" Jocelyn set the container down on the hearth and began to crumple up the sheets.

"Because when I do something that I've done before, it feels—" he struggled to express his feelings and settled on "—right. As if my body recognizes the action, even if my mind doesn't. And I get no impressions at all with the paper."

"Paper can't hurt," she said. "At least, I doubt it can."

"Wouldn't think so." He knelt beside her and began to carefully arrange the paper and small pieces of kindling in the fireplace. As Jocelyn watched, he took one of the long fireplace matches from the box on the mantel and struck it. the paper caught at once and within minutes the kindling was alight.

Carefully he positioned larger logs on top of the blaze and then rocked back on his heels and gave her a grin.

"A fire," he announced.

Jocelyn's heart twisted with tenderness at his pleased expression. He looked as if he'd just discovered fire.

"All we need now are some marshmallows," he said.

"Marshmallows!" she repeated as she suddenly realized that in all her rushing around to try to arrange everything, she hadn't once thought of food. And from the barren look of the kitchen, Lucas had cleaned out the food when he'd left last spring.

"Stick with me, kid, and I'll throw in chocolate bars and graham crackers, too." Lucas grinned at her.

"Not unless you're a magician," she muttered. "I completely forgot to get any food. Mother Hubbard would have been right at home here."

"I would assume that there's a grocery store around

somewhere,'' Lucas said. ''Besides, it's nice to know that you aren't perfect.''

''What do you mean?'' Jocelyn asked, taken aback.

''So far, you're the one who's arranged everything. The one who's taken care of all the details while I've just kind of gone along for the ride. I was beginning to feel like so much excess baggage.''

''Administrative assistants are supposed to be efficient,'' she said. ''And nornmally I am.''

''And normally I'm not deadweight,'' he replied. ''I certainly didn't mean that as a criticism. I'm sure you're very efficient. I'm also sure that I didn't marry you because of your efficiency.''

Jocelyn blinked, not sure what to say. She most emphatically didn't want to dwell on the fictitious reasons for their bogus marriage. ''Being organized is very important to me,'' she said, sticking to a neutral subject.

''Why?'' he asked.

''Why?''

''That was the question. Why is being organized so important to you?''

Jocelyn bit her lip, wishing that she'd kept her mouth shut. One thing she hadn't counted on with this so-called marriage was that she had given Lucas the right to ask personal questions. And refusing to answer them was bound to make him suspicious.

''I guess because it gives me a feeling of being in control, and that is very important to me.'' She gave him part of the truth. ''And now that you've got the fire going, you need to rest.''

''I'm not tired,'' he repeated.

''But your head hurts, doesn't it?'' Jocelyn eyed his pale face narrowly.

''Just a little,'' he conceded.

"Okay, let's compromise. You lie down for an hour, and then we'll go buy food and some casual clothes."

"I accept. I'll rest for an hour, but not one second more, and you won't nag me to go to bed early and—"

"I am not nagging!"

"Pester me to go to bed early," he amended. "Do we have a deal?" He held out his hand.

Jocelyn stared down at it, longing to touch it. To place a kiss on the palm of his hand, to rub her cheek over it, to...

"Either accept the terms offered or make a counterproposal," Lucas said.

"I accept." She took his hand, trying to appear casual. It didn't work. The moment his hand closed over hers, she felt tiny pinpricks of awareness race along her nerve endings. They seemed to electrify the hairs on her arms and put her whole nervous system on red alert.

"This doesn't seem familiar," Lucas muttered, and Jocelyn froze in sudden fear.

"What do you mean?" she asked cautiously.

"I mean shaking your hand just doesn't feel right. Not like when I talk to you. That feels natural, but shaking your hand doesn't."

"Probably because we haven't shaken hands all that often...whereas, we talk all the time," she said truthfully.

Lucas gave her a blinding smile in which devilment and relief were equally mixed. "Of course, I should have thought of that myself. Married couples don't go around shaking hands, do they?"

Jocelyn blinked, trying to pull her attention away from the intoxicating effect of his smile long enough to focus on what he was saying.

"This is what would be familiar." Lucas reached out

and enfolded her in his arms. Pulling her close, he lowered his head and placed a swift kiss on her surprised mouth.

Shock waves of pleasure ran through her, short-circuiting her thought processes.

She wasn't sure even in her own mind whether she was glad or not when he immediately released her and stepped back. If a casual kiss affected her like that, how would she react if he were to make love to her? she wondered. The thought was mind-boggling. One thing was certain—the next week or so was going to be a journey into unknown emotional waters. Waters that could turn treacherous once Lucas regained his memory.

For a moment Jocelyn doubted the wisdom of what she was doing. Her doubt died when she looked at Lucas's dear face. No matter what the cost to herself emotionally, she couldn't turn her back on him. He needed her, and she loved him. Nothing else mattered besides those two facts.

# *Chapter Four*

Jocelyn carefully eased open the lodge's bedroom door and peered inside. To her relief, Lucas was stretched out on the bed sound asleep.

Hungrily her eyes traced over his body, lingering on the rhythmic rise and fall of his wide chest. The very regularity of the movement helped to calm her fears, which were never far from the surface since the accident. There was nothing to worry about, she told herself. The doctor had reassured her that Lucas had sailed through the operation in excellent physical shape. There was no reason for her to panic every time he was quiet.

So why did she? She tried to analyze her reaction in the hope of conquering it.

Because she loved him past the point of reasoning, she finally decided. She was petrified, even now, that the doctor might have missed something. That there would be an unexpected complication and Lucas would suddenly die. The fact that intellectually she knew her fears were illogical didn't make the slightest difference to her emotions. She still felt that way.

Jocelyn stifled a sigh. Her hidden fears would have to remain exactly that—hidden. She couldn't allow Lucas to see them. His memory loss was enough for him to cope with. He shouldn't have to deal with her fears, too.

Silently she stepped back and closed the door behind her. Lucas probably wouldn't stay asleep long, so she'd better take advantage of the time to get a few things done.

Jocelyn retrieved her purse from where she'd dumped it on the couch, pulled out a notepad and, using the portable phone beside the couch, called the office.

Richard must have been expecting her call, because she was put through to him immediately. Succinctly she told him about Lucas's amnesia, impressing on him the absolute necessity of not telling anyone about it. Not only might it undermine their customers' confidence, if they found out that the head of the company didn't remember a thing about the company, but it was imperative that neither Lucas's stepmother nor his half brother find out.

To her relief, Richard wholeheartedly agreed with her. Not only was he genuinely fond of Lucas, but close acquaintance with Bill and his greedy mother over the years had given him an implacable mistrust of them.

After promising to provide him with regular updates on Lucas's condition, Jocelyn hung up. Her second call was to the answering machine in her apartment. She was lulled into a false sense of security as she worked her way through several calls from telemarketers, four invitations to holiday parties from friends and a message from the library telling her that the book she'd put on reserve was in. It was a security which was abruptly shattered when she reached the last message and heard Bill's voice demanding to know why she hadn't called him with a progress report on her search for the will.

Jocelyn took several deep, steadying breaths, reminding herself that Bill's ability to cause mayhem in her life was at an end. Having given her notice to Lucas meant that Bill's threats were meaningless. There wasn't anything more he could do to her.

Jocelyn stared blindly at the pale-beige wall in front of her as she tried to figure out what Bill might do if she simply ignored his message.

It would probably increase his sense of being treated badly, she finally decided. And he would try to do something about it. Chances were he wouldn't have any trouble finding out that she and Lucas had gone on a business trip to Buffalo. There had been no reason to keep the trip a secret.

Once Bill started backtracking their movements, he would find out about the accident. It wouldn't take a Sherlock Holmes to figure out that Lucas was probably recuperating at his ski lodge and that she was with him. And once Bill found that out, he could well decide to come to Vermont and threaten her in person. Her stomach twisted at the thought. Bill at a distance was hard to deal with. Bill up close was a nightmare.

It would be far better to stall him, she decided. To make him think that she was cooperating with him, so he'd stay where he was and leave them alone until Lucas was better.

But what could she say? She stared down at the phone as she tried to think. Something neutral. Something that would allow him to read anything into the message he wanted to.

But she shouldn't call from either Lucas's phone or her cell phone, she decided. Bill surely had caller ID, and he would immediately know where she was. She wanted to postpone his learning that bit of information as long as possible.

She'd call him from a pay phone when they went into town, she decided. Pay phones wouldn't register on caller ID. At least, she didn't think they would.

"What's the matter?"

Lucas's voice made her jump, and Jocelyn jerked around to find him standing in the doorway. His dark hair was slightly rumpled, but his face seemed more relaxed than it had been. As if he'd managed to throw off the exhaustion caused by the plane trip up here.

"Nothing," she hastily said.

"Then why do you look so worried? Who are you talking to?" His eyes dropped to the phone, still in her hand.

Jocelyn quickly set it down.

"I was just checking the messages on my answering machine at work," she said.

"And that makes you look like you'd just lost your last friend?" he asked skeptically.

"I haven't lost you," she said. "You're right here."

Lucas ignored the sudden warmth he felt from her words, concentrating instead on how she looked. She had seemed worried. Very worried. Something was wrong.

"You're avoiding the issue," he said.

"And you're imagining things." Jocelyn kept her voice light with an effort.

"Any messages of interest?" he asked, almost certain she was hiding something, but knowing there wasn't any way to force the issue. Something was going on that she didn't want him to know about, and he didn't have a clue what it was.

It could simply be that she didn't want to worry him. Or the reason for her reticence could be more ominous.

He remembered his earlier fears about the health of his marriage. Perhaps…

No. He ruthlessly chopped off his line of thought. He absolutely couldn't start reacting to something that might only exist in his mind. If he fell into that trap, he could well create problems in his marriage where none had been before. The only thing he could do at present was to go along with what she was telling him.

"No." Jocelyn struggled to keep the relief she felt at his change of subject out of her voice. She hated lying to him, even if it was for his own good. Nor was she very good at it. Although, considering the amount of practice she was getting, she ought to be an expert by the time this was over, she thought ruefully.

"Just a few invitations to holiday parties. Oh, and I called Richard. He said that the office is very quiet. The only activity was that Amalgamated increased their quarterly order by thirty percent."

Lucas frowned slightly, trying to connect the name to something in his memory. He couldn't.

"Can we do it?" he finally asked.

"Sure, no problem. Richard's already set it in motion. He's doing it on voluntary-overtime basis, which, at this time of year, a lot of people are happy to get."

"Did you tell him about my…" Lucas grimaced and gestured toward his head.

"Amnesia," Jocelyn filled in. "Yes, I thought it best, but he'll keep it to himself. He doesn't think it would be good for business if it got out. Besides, just about the time the story would make the rounds, you'd be better and then we'd have to spend all our time assuring everyone you're back to normal."

"Promises, promises," Lucas said, and Jocelyn's heart contracted at his bleak expression.

"Promises backed up by experience. Your injury really isn't unique," she deliberately kept her voice matter-of-fact, when what she really wanted to do was throw her arms around him and comfort him. But she knew the best way to keep Lucas from worrying himself to death was to convince him that she honestly believed he would get better. That his amnesia was nothing more than a temporary inconvenience.

"So you keep saying," he muttered.

"And I'll keep on saying it until you believe me. Although I imagine you'll get your memory back before then. You really are a very stubborn man."

Lucas looked down his nose at her and said, "The word is *determined,* woman."

"A rose by any other name." Jocelyn felt her spirits rise at the gleam of laughter she could see in his eyes.

Lucas watched her soft lips curve upward and felt an overwhelming urge to kiss them.

Why not? he thought. He was married to her. That blasted doctor might have banned making love for some reason that made no sense to him, but there couldn't be anything wrong with just kissing her.

Giving in to the impulse, he sat down on the sofa beside her and gathered her in his arms. His eagerness suffered a momentary setback when he felt her tense. Why would she tense at his touch? he wondered uneasily. Why...

His train of thought was quickly derailed as the faint fragrance of the perfume she was wearing drifted toward him. She smelled of flowers, of springtime. The intoxicating scent made rational thought impossible.

Instinctively his arms tightened, wanting her closer to him. The warmth and softness of her breasts pressing into his chest sent the blood pounding through his veins.

Blindly, driven entirely by instinct, he lowered his

head, his mouth finding hers. Her lips felt every bit as soft as they looked and tasted even better.

If it felt this good just to kiss her, what had it felt like when he'd made love to her? he wondered distractedly. He felt the touch of her fingertips on his cheek like a brand, and his arms tightened convulsively. He traced over her lower lip with the tip of his tongue, wanting, needing closer physical contact.

Jocelyn shivered and her reaction escalated his excitement. It also sent a sudden shaft of pain lancing through his head.

He instinctively froze, afraid to move for fear of making the pain worse.

Sensing something was wrong, Jocelyn struggled free from the web of sensual desire his kiss had plunged her into and leaned back, studying his suddenly pale face.

"Your head hurts." She made the words a statement, not a question.

Gently, she slipped out of his arms leaving him feeling bereft.

Lucas forced a grin and said, "I've heard of using a headache as an excuse for avoiding sex but this is the first time I've ever heard of lovemaking causing one."

"Kissing must come under the heading of stress." Jocelyn struggled to get control of her emotions. It wasn't easy. His kiss had sent them into wild disarray.

"Or, more likely, excitement," Lucas said, "because kissing you is incredibly exciting."

Jocelyn felt a flare of happiness at his words, which she struggled to extinguish with common sense. His compliment was meaningless, because he didn't have any memory of other kisses to compare it with. But even so, it was a dream come true—that for a few days Lucas thought she was sexy. Sexy and desirable. Her heart lifted.

"The pain's already gone," Lucas told her. "It wasn't really a headache. More like a sudden stab that faded just as quickly as it came."

"You're sure?" She eyed him worriedly. "You don't want to take something for it?"

"What I want to do would undoubtedly bring it back," he said dryly. "Weren't we going to go into town after my nap?"

"Yes." Jocelyn relaxed as she watched the color return to his lean cheeks. "We need to get some casual clothes and food."

"Then let's get on with it."

Jocelyn watched as Lucas got to his feet and carefully closed the glass doors to the fireplace. Then he peered down at the ceramic tile around the front of the fireplace before he ran his hand over the carpeting.

"What are you doing?" Jocelyn asked curiously.

"Making sure that no stray sparks landed on the carpet. Sparks can smolder for quite a while before bursting into flames, and I don't want to burn the place down while..." He paused as he realized what he was saying.

"It must be my subconscious telling me what to do," he finally said. "Because I don't remember ever having done this before, but I automatically did it."

"Your subconscious coupled with your basic sense of survival," Jocelyn agreed. "That's a pretty well-developed instinct in most people."

"Interesting," Lucas murmured. "At any rate, the carpet has no hot spots and the embers can't cause any trouble behind that glass screen. So it's safe to go. By the way, exactly where is this town we're going to?"

"I haven't a clue. All I want is a place that is big enough to have a grocery and a clothing store. Do you have any feelings about it?"

Lucas tried to retrieve something from his memory and failed.

"Don't worry," she said. "We'll pick a direction and head that way. Sooner or later we have to come to civilization."

"It's the 'later' that worries me," he said. "The road looked pretty desolate coming in. Just a few scattered gas stations and the occasional bar."

"Yes, it was," she said slowly. "So let's continue on down the road, since we know we aren't going to find anything back the way we came."

"Sounds logical to me. Can I drive?"

"No! Tomorrow, if you want to, you can try backing up and down the driveway and see how that feels," she said, moderating her refusal.

"Probably like I'm fifteen and playing with my father's car," he said dryly, and then blinked as an image of a gray-haired man suddenly filled his mind. The man's expression was furious, but what he was furious about or even with whom he was furious, Lucas didn't know. Like so many other things he didn't know, he thought in frustration.

Although, maybe his subconscious had pulled the picture out of his mind in response to his comment about his father's car. Maybe that was a picture of his father. If so, he certainly hadn't appeared to be the long-suffering type of parent.

"You said my parents were dead?" He vaguely remembered her telling him that when he'd been at the hospital.

"Yes, your mother died when you were just a little boy, and your father died five, almost six years, ago."

"Of what?" Lucas asked.

Jocelyn shook her head. "The cause was never mentioned that I remember. I would assume it was a heart attack. You could ask Richard. He'd know.''

Lucas shook his head. ''It hardly matters now. I just wondered. Let's go.''

''Good idea,'' she agreed. ''I want to get back before dark, if possible. These narrow, winding roads aren't going to be much fun to navigate in the dark.''

Lucas waited for some kind of internal response to her words and got exactly nothing which made him wonder if either they weren't all that bad or he was so used to driving over them that they didn't worry him. Or maybe all it meant was that his subconscious was on strike.

Frustrated, Lucas retrieved his coat from the chair where he'd dropped it.

Jocelyn got her coat out of the closet beside the front door. He frowned as he watched her button it up. She needed a thick, down parka, warm gloves, a wool hat and cashmere scarf. That coat might be fine for the city, where she wasn't outside for long, but up here she would quickly freeze. She looked so delicate with her slight figure. Rather like a garden fairy. A sexy garden fairy. And he wanted to keep her looking like that and not like an ice fairy.

''Ready?'' she asked, her happiness at being in his company adding a lilt to her voice.

''As I'll ever be.'' He followed her out of the house, pausing to lock the door. He'd have to see about getting her a key of her own, he decided. He didn't like the idea of her not being able to get into the house by herself.

Once they were on the road, he pulled his wallet out of his pocket and started counting the bills in it.

''What are you doing?'' Jocelyn took her eyes off the narrow road long enough to give him a quick glance.

"Counting up our resources for this shopping trip. I have exactly three hundred and seventy-two dollars."

"Don't worry about it, I have a credit card. We'll use that and save the cash for emergencies."

"Credit card?" he repeated and looked back into his wallet. "So do I. Two, in fact." He pulled out a platinum American Express and a Mastercard.

"The American Express card is for business. Edward will get bent out of shape if you use it for something not business related. Edward is your head accountant," she explained at his blank look.

"And this isn't business," he agreed.

Not unless you count funny business, Jocelyn thought on a flash of guilt.

"Don't worry, your other card has an almost unlimited line of credit on it."

Lucas's dark brows shot up. "I take it we have money with that much credit?"

"The one does not necessarily follow the other," she said dryly. "Credit is often given with no common sense involved. But in this case, you're right. You can buy most anything that takes your fancy."

"I see," Lucas said slowly. "Then we can—"

He broke off as something large and brown suddenly bounded out of the underbrush and darted across the road.

Jocelyn slammed on the brakes. "Bambi's father as I live and breathe. And it's a good thing he's quick, or he wouldn't be. Breathing, I mean."

"Fortunately, you're a good driver," Lucas said. "Those deer are a positive menace."

Jocelyn felt a glow of pleasure at his praise.

"They're graceful, though," she said.

"So's an arrow in flight, but that doesn't mean I want to be in its path."

"I'll just be more careful now that I've been warned, so to speak."

She started forward at a slightly slower speed, her eyes constantly scanning the underbrush for more wildlife. To her relief she didn't find any. What she did find was more and more houses.

"The area appears to be more built up here." Lucas's words echoed her own observation.

"We should find a shopping center or a small town pretty soon."

Five minutes later she was proved right when she rounded a curve in the road to find herself on the outskirts of a picturesque village.

"Looks like something out of travel brochure," she observed as she slowly navigated the main street. "Keep an eye out for likely looking stores, and I'll turn around at the end of the village and come back."

Lucas obediently took note of a promising looking sporting-goods store and a restaurant. Jocelyn turned around in the parking lot of a grocery store and then went back to park in front of the sporting-goods store.

"We should be able to get clothes in here," she said. "Then we can pick up some groceries before we head back."

"Clothes first, then into the restaurant for a meal before the grocery store." Lucas said. "You've had a tiring day, both physically and mentally. I don't want you to have to fix us a meal once we get back, and I have no idea if I can cook."

Jocelyn felt a glow of happiness at the concern in his voice. It felt so odd to have someone worried about her well-being. Odd and very seductive.

"I accept," she said as she followed Lucas into the store.

They had no more than walked in when a gorgeous blonde who looked as if she spent her free time skimming over the slopes pounced on them.

"May I help you?" The woman gave Lucas a slow smile that raised Jocelyn's blood pressure. How dare she come on to Lucas like that when she was standing right here?

"We're just looking at the moment," Jocelyn said shortly.

The woman gave Jocelyn a cursory glance, gave Lucas another seductive smile and said, "Be sure to call me if I can be of any help."

Turning, she sauntered off, her trim hips swaying in their skintight pants.

Jocelyn shot a surreptitious glance at Lucas, relaxing slightly when she saw he was studying the store, not the woman's sexy walk. But then, he never had responded to any of the blatant invitations he'd received when she'd been with him, she remembered. Lucas was not a man who liked being chased. The realization made her relax slightly.

"Where do we start?" Lucas asked.

Jocelyn glanced at the smudges the wood he'd carried had left on the front of his dress coat and said, "Jackets."

"And hats, gloves and scarves," he added. "Bright red, I think."

"You'd look good in red," Jocelyn said with an appreciative glance at his dark coloring.

"Not for me, for you. I can ski."

Jocelyn examined his words but couldn't arrange them into a sequence that made any sense. "Is red some kind of novice color everyone recognizes?"

"No, it's a bright color that is easy to see if you manage

to land in a snowbank and need to be dug out. Unless you can ski?''

''Nope, I've never tried it,'' she told him truthfully. Children who were raised in foster care were rarely given the opportunity to learn a hobby as expensive as skiing. And since she'd left foster care she'd been working and spending all her free time getting her bachelor's degree in business.

''I'll teach you.'' He headed toward a rack of long skis. ''You said I spent every free moment up here skiing, so I must be pretty good at it.''

''I also said the doctor was very emphatic about not doing anything that might cause another blow to your head. If you were to fall...'' Jocelyn shuddered at the very thought.

''My amnesia might become permanent.'' Lucas drew his own conclusions.

''I don't know.'' Jocelyn squashed the impulse to try to scare him for his own good. She was telling enough lies. ''The doctor wasn't specific, just emphatic. So please don't even think about skiing until you get a clean bill of health from him.''

''You're probably right,'' he said, giving the rack of skis one last, regretful look. ''It'd be stupid to risk reinjury at this date.''

Jocelyn relaxed slightly. One thing the accident hadn't changed was Lucas's basic personality. He had always been reasonable when presented with facts. He never sulked or moaned about what was, he simply dealt with it. It was one of the many things she loved about him.

''But I still want to buy you a red jacket,'' he insisted. ''I won't be one of the walking wounded forever. And when I can, I want to teach you to ski.''

''Sure,'' Jocelyn agreed. Red wasn't a color she usually

wore, and she knew full well that once he regained his memory, there wouldn't be any skiing lessons, but that was then, this was now. And now it would make Lucas happy if she bought a red jacket. That was enough for her.

Half an hour later she was the possessor of not only a new jacket, but a whole wardrobe suitable for weekends in the country. Lucas had ignored her tentative attempts to limit his purchases, pointing out that they might be here for weeks and she would need everything he was buying. The seductive thought of spending weeks pretending to be Lucas's wife was enough to momentarily hold her in thrall, and by then it was too late. Lucas had handed over his credit card and she could hardly get into an argument in front of a clerk.

They stashed their purchases in the Mercedes' trunk and decided to walk the half block to the restaurant. As they crossed the street, Jocelyn noticed the pay phone on the corner in front of the drugstore. It was exactly what she needed to call Bill and stall him.

But how was she going to get away from Lucas long enough to make the phone call? she wondered, as she followed him into the restaurant. Maybe— An idea suddenly occurred to her as they waited for the hostess to seat them.

"Lucas, would you order me a hamburger, French fries and a cup of coffee. I want to run a prescription over to the pharmacy."

"Why don't we do it after we eat?"

"If I take it over now, then it will be filled and ready for us to pick it up when we're done. Otherwise we'll have to wait."

Lucas's first impulse was to say he'd go with her. For some reason, he didn't want to let her out of his sight. He knew it wasn't logical, but he felt better when he could see her, and absolutely fantastic when he could touch her. But maybe their enforced closeness was starting to irritate her. The disturbing thought occurred to him. Maybe she wanted a few minutes away from him.

Telling himself not to be selfish, he said, ''Sure, how do you like your hamburger cooked?''

''Well-done,'' she said. ''And I want lettuce, tomato and mayonnaise on it.''

''Okay. Don't be long. Cold French fries are disgusting.''

Jocelyn just smiled at him, relieved to have so easily gotten her way.

She hurried out the door and headed toward the drugstore.

Lucas moved to the window so he could watch her, frowning when she stopped at the pay phone at the corner and started putting change into it. What was she doing? he wondered. He knew she had a cell phone—he'd seen it when she'd taken a tissue out of her purse at the sporting-goods store. Why didn't she use it if she wanted to call someone? Why stand out in the cold to make a call?

The answer was obvious—because she didn't want him to overhear her. Whoever she was calling, she didn't want him to know about it. But why? He couldn't think of a single answer that didn't make him nervous. Especially when he remembered how tense she'd been when he'd taken her in his arms. Could his first fear have been right? Could their marriage be in trouble? Could she be involved with another man? But how could a marriage that was less than two months old be in trouble? Hell, she hadn't had time to get tired of him.

Lucas rubbed his forehead, which was beginning to ache from his speculations. And they were speculations, he reminded himself. Just because he couldn't think of an innocent reason for her preferring to use a pay phone over the house phone or her cell phone didn't mean there wasn't one.

"If you'll follow me, sir," the hostess said, and he reluctantly moved away from the window. Whatever Jocelyn's reason was, he had no intention of asking her about it for fear of what she might say. He didn't think he was ready to find out that his marriage had problems. Maybe he never would be.

Jocelyn waited nervously as the phone to Bill's penthouse rang. And rang. She breathed a sigh of relief when his answering machine kicked in. At least she was spared having to talk to him in person.

As soon as the beep sounded, she identified herself, told him she was working on the problem. Which was certainly true. If Bill was stupid enough to think that that meant she was caving in to his demands that wasn't her fault.

Feeling as if she'd once again managed to dodge the bullet, she hung up and hurried into the drugstore to drop off the prescription the doctor had given her for Lucas's headaches.

## *Chapter Five*

"Look at that." Lucas gestured to his right, and Jocelyn's grip on the steering wheel automatically tightened as she scanned the road looking for another suicidal deer.

She squinted, trying to penetrate the darkness that had fallen while they'd been in the grocery store.

"What did you see?" she asked.

"The lights on that house we just passed. There's some more right ahead."

"You mean the Christmas lights?"

"Yes."

"They are pretty at night," she agreed.

"I think I want some."

"But who's going to see them where you live?"

"Where *we* live," he corrected.

"You, we. It makes no difference. The lodge is still out in the middle of nowhere."

"I'll see them. I want Christmas lights," he repeated. "Lots of them.... Did you put up Christmas lights before we were married?" he asked.

"No, I always lived in apartments. It's hard to string lights outside when you're five stories up."

He chuckled. "Think of it as a challenge. But didn't you decorate when you were a kid?"

Jocelyn searched her memory. "Only one of the families I lived with hung Christmas lights outside, and then it was just the man and his sons who did them."

Lucas felt a gust of anger at the wistfulness he could hear in her voice. He couldn't do anything about the bleakness of her childhood memories, but he could certainly do something about her future Christmas holidays. Starting with this one.

"That was then, this is now," he said. "Now we are going to establish our own traditions, starting with lights."

Jocelyn bit her lip, feeling like bursting into tears. She wished with all her heart that what he was saying was true. That he really did love her. That they really were married and were going to establish their own traditions.

Taking her silence as agreement, he said, "First thing tomorrow we'll go back into town and get lights, and we can pick up anything we forgot."

"Forgot!" Jocelyn repeated incredulously. "Both the trunk and the back seat are loaded. We not only got everything we needed, we got a ton of stuff we don't need at all."

"If that is a reference to my ten-pound bag of jumbo shrimp..."

"Now, why would you think that?" she said dryly.

"I think I like shrimp," he insisted.

"You'd better, because I sure don't like it ten pounds worth."

"We can barbecue them over the open fireplace tomorrow night along with the marshmallows," he said.

Jocelyn grimaced. ''Are you aware that the last thing the nurse said to me before I checked you out of the hospital was to make sure you ate a healthy diet?''

''One should aim for a healthy diet over a period of time, not for every meal.'' The words popped out of his mouth, catching him by surprise. He didn't know if that was something he knew or if he had just made it up on the spot because it sounded good.

''Perhaps, but at this rate you're going to have to eat healthily for the rest of the year just to balance what you bought today. One really doesn't need four different flavors of ice cream.''

''Speak for yourself. What do we normally buy in the way of food?'' Lucas asked curiously. He thought it odd that he had gotten absolutely no flashes of memory about anything as he'd worked his way through the grocery store with Jocelyn. Unless it was a job that he usually left to her. Did they have a division of labor when it came to household chores?

''Eat?'' Jocelyn repeated, trying to think of what to say. She'd eaten with him lots of times, both at restaurants and from delis when they'd been working late at the office, but she had never been to his apartment. For all she knew, he could be in the habit of microwaving TV dinners every evening. But then, he didn't know what he normally prepared, either, she remembered.

''Mostly stuff that's quick to fix.''

''I take it I work long hours,'' he said, weighing her words. It didn't sound as if they had much time to themselves.

''You've been putting in some long hours finalizing the Blefford deal,'' she confirmed.

Was that the cause of the reticence he could feel in her? he wondered. Did she resent the fact that he spent so much time working instead of spending it building a relationship with her? But she was his assistant. She had to have known how he worked before she married him. Unless he'd promised to ease up once they were married and, for some reason, he'd reneged on his word?

Which seemed hard to believe. Anyone lucky enough to have a woman like Jocelyn as his wife should be happy to spend as much time with her as he could. So why hadn't he?

He didn't know, but whatever his behavior in the past, he would do things differently now, he decided. He would use this time at the lodge to try to forge a better relationship with her. To try to iron out those odd little vibes he kept getting.

"What other Christmas traditions shall we start?" he asked.

Deciding there was no harm going along with his plans, at least no more harm than she'd already incurred, Jocelyn said, "Christmas cookies. Lots of Christmas cookies."

"Definitely cookies," he agreed. "I put a vote in for chocolate chip."

"And decorated sugar cookies." Jocelyn got into the spirit.

"And let's make some from our ethnic backgrounds. Where does your family come from?" Lucas asked, insatiably curious about her.

"My mother is of Polish descent. I haven't a clue as to who my father is. My mother was very into doing her own thing, and that didn't include a husband." Despite her attempt to sound matter-of-fact, Jocelyn's voice reflected some of the pain she'd felt as a child.

"Where is she now?" Lucas asked.

"She died when I was thirteen. Alcohol was her drug of choice."

Lucas wanted to take her in his arms and drive out the pain he could hear in her voice, but she was driving. Nor did he have any idea what to say to banish it. The best thing to do was to try to make her present life better, so that all the good memories would crowd out the unhappy past.

"We'll do better by our children," he said comfortingly.

Jocelyn's breath caught in her lungs at the intoxicating thought of having Lucas's children—a boy with his eyes and maybe a girl with his gorgeous dark hair.

"How many did we plan on having?" he asked.

"How many?" His question took her by surprise.

"Didn't we discuss children?"

"We got married. We didn't negotiate a contract," she muttered, wondering how to get him off this subject. It was so close to her dreams that it was painful to talk about.

"Don't you want children?" he persisted.

"Yes, of course I do. I'd like kids."

"I think I do, too," he said tentatively and then added when the words felt exactly right, "I think an even half dozen."

"Think again!" she said.

"You said you liked kids."

"I did, and I do, but I don't want a horde. I want a couple, so I'll have time to do things with them."

"A couple hardly seems worth getting started for," Lucas muttered, reluctant to give up his mental image of a bunch of children with Jocelyn's bright features.

"I think this is just your accident speaking," she finally said. "Because you've never mentioned wanting all those kids before."

''Maybe my accident is just allowing my real thoughts to come to the surface,'' he said slowly.

Could well be, Jocelyn thought wryly. His accident was certainly allowing her to indulge her own deeply held desire to be Lucas's wife.

''Let's discuss this when you get your memory back,'' she finally said, not wanting to waste their precious time together arguing about kids that would never be born. At least, she wouldn't be the lucky woman to have them.

''Okay,'' he said, reluctantly dropping the subject. For some reason he had the feeling it was vitally important that he bind her to him with every emotional tie he could come up with.

Maybe his compulsion was a result of his accident, he thought, trying to soothe his jumpy nerves. Maybe his fears and uncertainties really were all in his head.

''I think...yes,'' Jocelyn murmured in satisfaction as she recognized the driveway leading to Lucas's lodge.

Carefully she steered the Mercedes up the driveway, stopping in front of the door. With everything they had bought, she didn't want to carry it any distance.

''I'll unload,'' Lucas said. ''You put things away.''

''But I don't know where anything goes,'' she objected.

''You think I do?''

''There is that,'' she admitted. ''How about if we both unload and both put things away? That way we'll both know where everything is.''

''Those sacks are heavy,'' he objected.

''Rein in your chauvinism. I may not be very big, but I'm certainly sturdy. I can carry a few bags of groceries.''

With both of them working, it didn't take long to unpack the car. Putting things away was harder. Finally Jocelyn simply opened every cabinet door in the small kitchen and started to shove supplies into them, promising herself she'd organize them tomorrow when she wasn't so tired.

"Are you hungry?" Lucas asked.

"No." Jocelyn took a good look at him, alerted by an odd sound in his voice. His features were pale and his lips were compressed as if his head was bothering him.

"Then I think I'll toast some marshmallows over the fire. At least, I will as soon as I manage to get it going again," he said.

"Your head hurts, doesn't it?"

"Just a little, nothing to get excited about."

"How about if you take some of your pain medication and then we can both toast marshmallows," she suggested.

"I don't like to take that stuff."

"I know, but if you don't, you're going to spend a wakeful night because that pain is going to cause all kinds of bad dreams. And then you'll be tired tomorrow. Not only that, but you can't heal as fast if you aren't sleeping well."

"I wouldn't want to disturb your sleep," he said slowly. Actually, he didn't want to do anything that might give her an excuse not to share his bed. Even if he couldn't make love to her, he could still hold her. Just the thought of having her snuggled up beside him made him willing to agree to anything, including the doctor's overly conservative view of medicine.

Disturb her sleep? The comment hit Jocelyn with the force of a blow. Did he expect her to share the lodge's only bedroom? More disturbingly, the lodge's only bed? But then, why wouldn't he expect it? she answered her own question. She had told him they were married. Married couples routinely shared a bed. And he had agreed to the stipulation that they couldn't make love. What would be the harm of sharing his bed?

Do you want the short list or the long list? she asked herself, knowing that it would be terrible for her peace of mind to be so close to her heart's desire and yet so far away from it. But what was that old saying about half a loaf being better than none? Or was this situation covered under another old saying about being careful what you wish for because you may get it?

She stifled a grimace. All those old sayings proved was that there was one for every circumstance and half the time they contradicted each other.

"I'll take the medication," Lucas said. "Where is it?"

"I stuck it in my purse, but on second thought, maybe you'd better not take it until after we're finished toasting the marshmallows. I don't even want to think about what might happen if you were to get groggy around an open fire."

"I told you that stuff is dangerous," he muttered.

"Virtually every medication, including plain old aspirin, is dangerous when used irresponsibly," Jocelyn countered.

She picked up the oversize bag of marshmallows and looked around the small kitchen.

"What are you looking for?" Lucas asked.

"Something to toast marshmallows with. Any ideas?"

Lucas closed his eyes and waited to see if he got a flash of memory. Nothing came. Either he wasn't in the habit of toasting marshmallows or his memory wasn't in the mood to cooperate.

"Not a one," he finally said. "Haven't you ever toasted them?"

"Nope, I never had an opportunity to join the Girl

Scouts, and none of the families I lived with had a fireplace or were into camping.''

Opening a kitchen drawer, she poked around inside it and finally pulled out a wicked-looking two-pronged fork.

''How about this?'' she asked.

''As a weapon it looks formidable. What is it?''

''A meat fork. It should be long enough to protect our hands from the fire. We can share.''

''Sounds good to me. I'll have the fire up to speed in a few minutes.''

Jocelyn picked up the marshmallows and followed him into the living room. Setting them down on the hearth, she got his prescription out of her purse and set it on the end table beside the couch so that she wouldn't forget to remind him to take it. She had no doubt that if she didn't, he would conveniently forget.

Her eyes lingered on his intent features as he carefully fanned the coals in the fireplace into blazing life. He was so determined not to be dependent on drugs and, while she admired his resolve in the abstract, she also knew that there were times when a person had to admit that he couldn't do everything himself. That he or she needed help.

''There,'' he said in satisfaction as the fire flared up. ''Bring on the marshmallows.''

Jocelyn tore open the bag, stuck one on the end of the fork and handed it to him.

He carefully held it out to the fire, jumping slightly when the whole thing burst into flame. As Jocelyn watched, it quickly turned black and fell off the fork into the fire.

''Hmm,'' she said. ''Think I need to push the marshmallow down a little more. Good thing we bought the big bag.''

Taking a second one, she jammed it well down on the fork and held it out to him. He cautiously held it out to the fire, being careful not to let it catch fire this time.

"How do you like yours done?" he asked.

"Never having had one, I'm approaching this without any prejudices."

Lucas gave her a sidelong glance and murmured, "Is that the way you approach all new experiences?"

Jocelyn's breath caught in her throat at the sparkle she could see in his eyes. She didn't have the slightest doubt that the conversation had just shifted from marshmallows to something far more seductive. And dangerous. She took a deep breath to try to slow her rising heart rate.

She was about to try to turn the conversation to something unemotional when she realized that if she continually tried to stop all his attempts at light lovemaking, he would be bound to wonder what was wrong. And that would create the very kind of stress she was supposed to avoid.

Or was she simply rationalizing doing what she really wanted to do, which was to get close to him? She wasn't sure.

But simply because she wasn't sure of her own motivation didn't make her conclusion any less valid. Trying to keep Lucas at an arm's length emotionally would be stressful for him. She needed to find a balance between normal married behavior and behavior that she could justify once he regained his memory. Not an easy task, she conceded. Especially not given that she had very little practice at emotional relationships of any kind.

"Damn!" Lucas's muttered expletive distracted her, and she was only too glad to abandon her tangled thoughts.

"What's wrong?" she asked.

Lucas vigorously blew out the flaming marshmallow, eyed its charcoal exterior critically and finally said, "You want to try the well-done version first?"

"I'm game." Jocelyn held out a hand for the fork.

"Be careful," he said as he handed it to her. "The inside is boiling hot."

Jocelyn carefully nibbled the outside and then blew on the interior until it was cool enough to eat.

"I like it," she said. "The charcoal adds a certain crunchy piquant flavor."

"Want another one?" he asked.

"After you've had one," she said.

Lucas squeezed another marshmallow onto the fork and held it over the fire.

"When we get the outdoor decorations tomorrow, we'll have to see about getting some longer forks."

"Longer forks," Jocelyn repeated, automatically filing his request on her mental to-do list.

"And birdseed," she said.

"Birdseed?" Lucas peered down at the marshmallow he was toasting. "Chocolate with them might be good, but birdseed?"

"For the birds, not us," she said. "There was the cutest little chickadee outside when we arrived today. I wonder what they eat?"

"Don't start feeding the birds unless you are going to continue through the winter. They become dependent on you and can starve if you suddenly leave," Lucas stated.

Jocelyn blinked. "Really?"

Lucas frowned. "I'm not sure. I just opened my mouth and that came out. I have no idea if it's true or not."

True or not, his ability to come up with relevant information had to mean that Lucas was in the process of regaining his memory, she realized. A sense of urgency suddenly gripped her. How much longer would she have with him before his memory returned and he knew that not only wasn't she his wife, she wasn't even his trusted assistant anymore.

Grimly she shoved the panicky feeling to the back of her mind. It hadn't happened yet, and until it did there was no sense in worrying about it. Worrying about the inevitable never stopped it from happening. It simply spoiled the time you had before it did happen.

"That sounds reasonable," she said slowly. "Maybe we can find a book on feeding birds while we're hunting down decorations and forks. We can..." She paused as she was suddenly overwhelmed by a yawn.

"You're tired. Why didn't you say something?" Lucas demanded.

"I'm not all that tired." She spoiled her denial by yawning again.

"I should have realized it myself," he said in chagrin. "You were the one who did all the work today, and I'm the one who took all the naps."

"You're also the one who just got out of the hospital this morning after having had major surgery," she reminded him.

"It's time for bed," he announced. "We're going to have a busy day putting up decorations tomorrow.

"You can have the first shower," he offered.

"Thanks." Jocelyn got to her feet and headed into the bedroom to get her nightgown. But no robe, she suddenly remembered. She never bothered with one when she was traveling because it only took up space in her suitcase and no one ever saw her in her hotel room. Well, at least her nightgown had been chosen for warmth and not glamour. Lucas would have to be madly in love with her to find her flannel gown sexy. And he wasn't, she reminded herself grimly. He hadn't even seemed to like her anymore once she'd resigned.

Pausing in the bedroom door, she turned.

"Don't forget to take your medicine," she reminded him.

"I won't."

"Good, I won't be long. I wonder how much hot water this place has?"

Lucas shrugged. "I would assume that I originally bought a water heater big enough for company."

"Probably." Jocelyn headed into the bathroom. She wanted to hurry with her shower. Then while Lucas was taking his, she could check the messages on her apartment phone and see if Bill had responded to her earlier call. With even a minimal amount of luck, Lucas would never hear her while the water was running.

Fifteen minutes later she emerged from the small bathroom, swathed from neck to toes in pale-pink flannel.

Lucas's eyebrows rose at the sight of her.

"You don't trust me to keep you warm?" he asked.

"Umm, it's not that," Jocelyn muttered. "It's just that I get cold easily."

To her relief he didn't pursue the topic. Instead he headed to the bathroom.

Jocelyn waited until she heard the sound of running water and then grabbed the phone. Hurriedly she dialed her home phone number and retrieved her messages. She skipped one from a firm trying to sell her vinyl siding, barely listened to one from a friend asking her if she wanted to go shopping in New York City the following Saturday, and then felt her skin crawl as she heard the sound of Bill's voice.

It was clear that Bill was not a happy camper. He wanted to know why she hadn't found the will yet. Then he added a variety of threats about what he was going to do if she didn't produce some results soon, and ended with a demand to know why she wasn't answering her phone, that trying to avoid him wasn't going to work.

Jocelyn flipped off her phone and stared blindly down at it, trying to figure out how to stall Bill long enough to give Lucas a chance to regain his memory.

Bill wanted a new will. What would happen if she were to give him a forged will? she wondered. He would probably think it was real and run to a lawyer to do whatever it was one did with wills. It might take months before the fact that it was really a fake came out. By that time Lucas would be back to normal.

Bill would be livid at having been duped, which was a plus as far as she was concerned. But Lucas might be pretty angry as well, she conceded. He was a proud man, and he wouldn't like the publicity a supposed second will would bring. Not only that, but Lucas would have to spend a lot of money on lawyers' fees just countering Bill's claims.

Added to which, she had no idea how to go about getting a fake will written. She could hardly go to a lawyer and ask for one. Even if she tried to pass it off as an elaborate practical joke, no lawyer was going to risk his license doing something like that. Nor did she blame them. If she had her choice she wouldn't want to be mixed up in this mess, either.

"Damn!" she muttered under her breath. There had to be something she could do about Bill. Something that didn't involve breaking the law.

Silently Lucas paused in the doorway of the living room, frowning slightly as he studied Jocelyn. She was staring at the cell phone as if it were a snake that had bitten her. Her expression was an odd combination of fear and anger. Who had she been calling? he wondered. And what had they said that had gotten this reaction from her.

He felt a surge of anger at the thought of anyone upsetting her.

"Did we get a phone call?" He tried to sound no more than causally interested.

"No. I was simply checking my messages again, and a friend asked me to go to New York next weekend for Christmas shopping."

"Do you want to go?" he asked as an image of a huge Christmas tree, its lights sparkling in the darkness suddenly flashed through his mind. A memory from another holiday visit to New York City? he wondered, and then dismissed it as unimportant. What was important was that Jocelyn should feel free to go to New York if she wanted to.

"I don't mind," he said, trying very hard to sound as if he meant it emotionally as well as intellectually. He didn't want her to leave. Even for a day. The very thought gave him a panicky feeling.

"I can go another time," she said.

If she didn't want to go, then why had she looked so upset, he wondered. Unless what was bothering her had nothing to do with her friend's invitation. Could there have been a second message? One from someone else entirely. Could there be another man in her life?

He had a sudden memory of Jocelyn looking desperately unhappy and grimly determined. About what? Could she have been telling him that she wanted out of their marriage? Fear shook him.

Get a grip, Forester. He jerked his imagination up short. You've only been married two months. There hasn't been time for her to have found another man. It has to be something else that's bothering her. But what it could be was the question.

He rubbed his head as it responded to his anxiety by starting to throb.

"Your head is hurting again," Jocelyn said, noticing his action. "You took your medicine, didn't you?"

"Yes, I did, and yes, my head hurts. Come on, let's go to bed."

Jocelyn closed her eyes on the wave of longing that surged through her. She'd spent the past six months dreaming about going to bed with Lucas, and now she was going to actually do it. And instead of it being a wonderful experience, it was going to be torture, because she was going to have to hide what she really felt. She just hoped she was strong enough to do it.

# Chapter Six

Jocelyn twitched uncomfortably as a particularly persistent sunbeam tried to insinuate itself beneath her eyelids. Slowly she opened her eyes, squinting slightly at the bright sunlight that flooded the room. Tomorrow she was not only going to lower the blinds on the windows, but she would pull the curtains over them and pin the edges together. It was much too early to be roused from the most restful sleep she'd had in ages.

She blinked as she woke up enough to realize just why she felt so warm and safe. It was due to the large man sleeping beside her.

Jocelyn closed her eyes to better savor the feel of Lucas's hard muscles touching her from shoulder to thigh. It felt fantastic to be that close to him. Every bit as good as her imagination had painted it. Maybe even better. In her daydreams she hadn't taken into account the elusive scent clinging to him.

She took a deep breath to try to label it, and couldn't. It was too complex. Masculine was the closest she could come. There was just the faintest trace of the spicy cologne he normally wore combined with the clean, underlying scent of the man himself. It was an aroma that was uniquely Lucas.

It was also a scent that she was never going to smell again after a couple of weeks. The harsh reality dimmed her pleasure.

Cautiously she eased herself out of bed, not wanting to wake Lucas. He needed all the rest he could get.

She paused by the side of the bed for a moment to stare down at his beloved face. His dark, rumpled hair had fallen across his forehead, almost obscuring his scar.

Her eyes wandered down over his features, lingering on his emerging beard. She peered closer as the sunlight added a definite reddish cast to the stubble. How interesting, she thought. His hair didn't have any red in it, but his beard did. What about the hair on the rest of his body? Her eyes followed her thoughts down the length of him. Would the hair on his chest have that same reddish glint to it? She didn't know, but she'd sure like to find out. She wanted to know everything about him, right down to the exact makeup of every single cell in his body.

He turned slightly, muttering in his sleep, and Jocelyn froze. She certainly didn't want to be caught hanging over him like a love-struck teenager. She was old enough to behave like a mature, sophisticated woman. She stifled a sigh. The problem was she wasn't sophisticated. At all. In fact, sometimes she had the eerie feeling that she was still a six-year-old inside. And a frightened six-year-old at that!

This was not the time for self-psychoanalysis, she told herself as she silently retrieved her exercise outfit from her suitcase. Getting her muscles loosened up sounded like an excellent idea with what Lucas had planned. She had the feeling she was going to spend a good part of the day clinging to the roof of the house while she hung Christmas lights, because she certainly wasn't going to allow Lucas to do it. No matter what he said.

Hurrying into the bathroom, she hastily changed into her forest green yoga pants and tank top, shivering slightly at the morning chill. She hastily popped on an oversize, pale-pink sweatshirt and then went to check the heat. As she'd expected, Lucas had turned it down last night before they'd gone to bed. She turned it back up, made coffee and then returned to the living room to do her exercises.

She was almost finished with her yoga routine when she heard a sound behind her and turned her head.

Lucas was standing in the bedroom doorway. He had on a pair of the jeans he'd bought yesterday and a deep-royal-blue turtleneck that emphasized his dark hair and eyes. Her gaze lingered on the intoxicating masculine picture he presented. He looked gorgeous. Absolutely perfect. She just wished she had the right to abandon her yoga and engage in some really interesting exercise with him.

"What are you doing?" he asked curiously as he came into the room.

"Yoga."

Lucas stared at the pale-beige wall for a long moment, giving his mind a chance to come up with an image of her doing it before. It didn't cooperate.

"Why?" he finally asked.

"Exercise is good for you," she repeated what her doctor had said.

"Do I exercise with you?" he asked.

"No, you jog."

This time his mind supplied him with an image of him running. He seemed to be on the side of a road and there was a cold wind whistling around his ears. There was also a furiously yapping small white dog running beside him while in the distance he thought he could hear a plaintive feminine voice calling the dog. His mental image was nowhere near as appealing as Jocelyn's yoga inside a warm, cozy house.

"Do I know how to do what you're doing?" he asked.

"No." Jocelyn wasn't sure of her facts, but it seemed the safest answer. He'd never mentioned anything but running. And skiing.

"Running isn't going to be easy with all that snow on the ground."

"You can't run!" She hastily vetoed the idea. If he tried to run, he might fall. She didn't know how hard he would have to hit his head to cause further damage, but she had no intention of finding out the hard way.

"Until the doctor gives you a clean bill of health, you had better keep both your feet firmly on the ground at all times."

"Okay," Lucas agreed. "Maybe I could do what you're doing instead. It doesn't look all that hard." He watched as she came out of one pose and repositioned herself in another. "You just seem to sit there."

"*Seems* being the operative word. It's not quite as easy as it looks."

Lucas walked over to her and studied her. "You look like a peony in the outfit." His eyes traveled from the pink sweatshirt down the enchanting length of her long legs encased in their green stretch pants.

Jocelyn considered his words, trying to decide if they were a compliment or not. He hadn't sounded as if he were enamored of peonies. She stifled a sigh. Now if he'd called her a long-stemmed rose...

And if wishes were horses then beggars would ride.

Jocelyn remembered one of the favorite quotes of one of her many foster mothers. No matter how much she might want to be, she simply wasn't the kind of woman who made men think in terms of roses and moonlight and romantic assignments. She had long since reached the conclusion that a riveting sexual appeal was either something you were born with or not. And in her case, it was not.

"I'll bet I could do that," he said.

Kicking off his shoes, he sat down on the floor beside her.

"I think you'd better start with a less adventurous pose," she said.

"Nonsense," he scoffed. "That pose looks tame enough for somebody's grandmother."

With a suddenness that took her by surprise, Lucas rearranged his body into a reasonable counterfeit of the pose she was doing.

"See, I told you this wasn't all that hard."

"You haven't got it exactly right," she told him. "And I really don't think you should..."

Determined to share her exercise program, he tried bending his body a little more. For a second nothing happened, and then he let out a yelp and hastily abandoned the pose, sprawling on the floor.

Jocelyn jumped to her feet.

"What did you do?" she demanded.

"Paid the price for hubris," he muttered into the carpet.

"Forget your ego! What did you do to your body?"

Lucas rolled over and grinned up at her.

"Does this mean you don't love me for my mind?"

"Considering what you have been doing to your body recently, I'm not going to have that much left to love. Now, what did you do?"

"I'm not sure. I felt a hot, burning sensation that went from my neck down my back," he admitted.

Jocelyn grimaced. "You must have pulled something. Trying to exercise without warming up first is..."

"Stupid," he finished the sentence.

"Ill-advised."

"To say nothing of painful," he added dryly. "But I still think it looks easy. Like you aren't really doing anything at all."

"Didn't anyone ever tell you that looks could be deceptive?" she said.

He didn't need anyone to tell him that, he thought in frustration. Everything about the situation he found himself in was deceptive. Or rather, it was more than it seemed. Or less, he wasn't quite sure which. The only thing he was definite about was that there was something odd about their marriage, and she was only pretending that everything was okay. Probably because of his accident. And if that were the case, he wasn't sure he ever wanted to regain his memory. He could live without his memories. He wasn't so sure he could live without Jocelyn.

"Try moving your shoulders," Jocelyn ordered.

Lucas did, and barely suppressed a wince.

"Muscle pull," she confirmed.

"Now that you've diagnosed it, do you have a cure?" he asked.

"Normally I'd say one of the over-the-counter anti-inflammatories, but I don't think mixing anything with that prescription the doctor gave you is a good idea. I guess it's going to come down to which hurts more, your head or your shoulder."

"My head feels fine," he said. "Great, as a matter of

fact. And once I have a couple of cups of that coffee I can smell, it ought to be even better.''

Jocelyn dropped to her knees beside him.

''Maybe I should try massaging the soreness?'' she said hesitantly. She wasn't clear even in her own mind if her offer came from her almost compulsive desire to touch him or if it was fueled by the more altruistic motive of helping him. It didn't matter, she finally told herself. A massage would benefit him no matter what her motivation was.

''That sounds good,'' Lucas said cautiously, hoping that the sudden flare of intense excitement he'd felt wasn't apparent in his voice. He didn't want to scare her off. Although maybe the reason she seemed to avoid touching him was that she was afraid he'd get angry if she aroused him when they couldn't make love. It was possible, he thought as he considered the idea. But surely she would realize that he wouldn't hold her responsible for a restriction that the doctor had placed on them? Unless he was normally an unreasonable man giving to blaming other people for not getting his own way. The thought sent a chill through him.

Could that be responsible for her odd manner? Could she have married him and found out that he was a selfish man who didn't take other people's needs and wants into consideration? Could she be regretting the marriage because of that?

But how could he find out? If he was selfish, would he recognize his selfishness? And Jocelyn was hardly going to tell him. At least, she wouldn't while he was still recovering from his injury, because whatever was causing the tension in their marriage, it was clear she was very protective of him.

A faint jab of pain shot through his head, and he hastily

cut off his tortured speculations. He most emphatically didn't want to do anything which would bring his headache back in full force. He wanted to spend the day with Jocelyn. He wanted to create good Christmas memories for her, not wander around in the drug-induced haze that the medicine caused.

"Roll over," Jocelyn told him, and Lucas obediently rolled onto his stomach.

"Now, close your eyes and relax."

He closed his eyes, but the relaxing part was impossible. His entire body was tense with anticipation.

His breath caught as he felt her slender hands slip beneath his knit shirt.

"You don't have to take your shirt off," she said as she pushed it up over his torso. "I'll just work around it."

He gasped as she began to knead the tight muscles at the base of his neck with surprisingly strong fingers.

"I'm sorry," she said. "Does it hurt?"

Oh, it hurt all right, but not why and where she thought, Lucas thought with grim humor. It was all he could do not to roll over, grab her and kiss her senseless.

He gritted his teeth against the longings that filled him, mentally trying to separate the feelings she was causing into their separate components in the hope of diffusing them slightly. It was hopeless. Plain old lust drowned his every rational thought. All he wanted to do was make love to her.

Finally, when he had almost reached the end of his endurance, she rocked back on her heels and said, "Try to move your shoulders now."

Had her voice sounded slightly breathless? He tried to analyze the tone. Was it possible that she had felt even a fraction of the longing he had?

Lucas rolled over and stared up at her. There were two spots of pink burning on her cheekbones, and her eyes seemed to glitter with some suppressed emotion. But what emotion? he wondered in frustration. It could just as easily be annoyance at him for pulling his muscle.

"Try moving your shoulders," she repeated. "It should be easier."

Unable to stand it one second longer, Lucas reached up, grabbed her arm and tugged her down on top of him.

She landed across his chest with a muffled squeak of surprise, and he hastily wrapped her in his arms before she could escape.

Jocelyn opened her mouth to ask him what he was doing and closed it when the absolute inanity of the question occurred to her. It was obvious what he was doing. He was about to kiss her. The only question was what was she going to do. Retreat or enjoy it.

She felt his long fingers spear through her hair, cupping the back of her head. His fingers tightened, inexorably pulling her closer to him.

Shivers coursed through her as her eyes focused on his firm lips. She wanted this so much, and yet she was so afraid to really give in to her desire for fear of where it might lead.

It can only lead to a kiss, she rationalized. You aren't such a fool that someone can make love to you against your better judgment.

Unconsciously she relaxed slightly as Lucas pulled her down to him with a rough hunger that she found intoxicating. She didn't know why, but at the moment he wanted her. He couldn't fake the fact that he desired her. Not as close as they were to each other.

As her lips met his, she stopped thinking and started to

feel, allowing the emotions swirling through her free rein. Sensation after sensation crashed through her.

A tiny whimper of pleasure escaped her, and she felt his arms momentarily tighten before he suddenly released her and rolled away.

Getting to his feet, he walked over to the patio doors, where he stood for a long moment staring out at the brilliant morning sunlight.

Jocelyn struggled to regain control of her body, which felt boneless. It took several deep breaths before she could even form a coherent thought. And once she could, she wasn't sure what to think. Why had he kissed her in the first place? And why had he released her as suddenly as he'd taken her in his arms?

She stared at the rigid line of his back, her eyes traveling down over his flat hips and the long line of his strong legs. He looked tense. Was he tense because of the kiss they'd shared or was it something else entirely?

Jocelyn gave her head a tiny shake, scattering her futile speculations. There was no way she could know without asking him, and she couldn't do that. Asking a man who was supposed to be your husband if he was affected by your kiss would sound very strange. Even to someone who had lost his memory.

Just accept the kiss as a side benefit and get on with it, she told herself.

Slowly she got to her feet, still feeling slightly disoriented.

"Do you want me to make breakfast?" Lucas finally broke the silence.

Gratefully she followed his lead. She most emphatically didn't want to have to endure a postmortem on that kiss.

"What are you planning on fixing?" she asked.

"I thought I'd open the refrigerator and see what looked familiar," he said.

"Why don't you open the cabinet and make friends with a box of cereal instead? That sounds much safer than messing with the stove."

Lucas looked down his nose at her, trying not to stare at her soft lips, still swollen from his kiss.

"Don't you think I can cook anything?" he demanded.

Jocelyn thought a moment, gave him a quick grin that tugged at his heart and said, "No."

"You are missing a good bet here," he told her.

"How so?"

"You should tell me that I love cooking. That way you won't have to do any."

"I didn't buy any antacid pills yesterday," Jocelyn said dryly. "You are infamous around the office for burning things in the microwave. One shudders to think what you could manage to accomplish with an open flame."

Lucas blinked as an image of a small tray filled with burned chicken formed in his mind.

"Maybe this is the time to learn," he finally said. "It's not like I've got anything else on my mind. Hell, I've barely got a mind to have anything on!" A sense of panic momentarily overwhelmed him. "Suppose I never regain my memory?"

"According to the doctor, the chance of that happening is virtually nil."

"Doctors don't know everything," he argued.

"They know a lot more about medical matters than you do. You're probably just grumpy because your blood sugar is low. You'll feel better after breakfast."

It wasn't low blood sugar he was suffering from, he thought ruefully. It was acute sexual frustration, and the only way that feeling was going to go away was if he could make love to her. But it wasn't her fault that the doctor had denied them that outlet. In fact, from her response to his kiss, she must be feeling just as frustrated as he did. And he was making it worse by behaving like a spoiled brat. A sense of shame filled him. If he wanted to convince her that being married to him was a great idea, that wasn't the way to go about it.

"You're probably right," he said, forcing himself to sound cheerful. "I'll get out the cereal and juice while you get dressed."

"Give me ten minutes to shower and change."

Jocelyn gave him a quick smile and hurried back to the bedroom, intent on getting ready as soon as possible. She didn't want to waste a precious moment of their day.

She rushed through her shower in record time, and seven minutes later was back in the kitchen. She found Lucas sitting at the tiny table, drinking coffee and staring out the window.

She followed his glance but couldn't see anything.

"What are you looking at?" she asked.

"This feels all wrong."

He gestured toward the carefully arranged table with its two bowls, two glasses of orange juice and two bananas neatly set in the precise middle of the table.

"Looks great to me," she said.

"Thanks." He felt a brief glow of pleasure at her praise. "But it isn't how it looks that bothers me. It's how it feels and it feels...wrong," he said.

Jocelyn felt a brief chill. Had his subconscious realized that she wasn't supposed to be sharing his breakfast with him?

"How so?" she asked cautiously as she slipped into the chair across from him.

"Incomplete." He struggled to explain the feeling.

"Probably because you don't have a newspaper. You always read the local paper and the *Wall Street Journal* with your breakfast," she said, remembering his habit from their business trips.

"Don't you mind?" he asked uncertainly.

"No," she said honestly. "There is only so much time in the morning, and I like to read the paper, too.

"We can ask about local delivery if you like," she said. "There probably is one because you have a whole stack of papers under the sink waiting to be recycled."

"That's okay. Now that I know why it felt so odd, I don't mind. Unless you want a paper?"

"Giving up the news is no hardship," she said. "It tends to consist of who killed whom or who's about to kill whom. And, if you want to find out what's going on in the business world, you can always call Richard. He'd be able to tell you anything you might want to know."

"I could, but the problem is I don't even know what questions to ask or what to make of the answers I'd get. Hell, I might as well ask questions about bioengineering. The answers would make as much sense to me."

"Today," she agreed. "But that might not be true tomorrow. And definitely not by next month. Quit worrying. I promise you everything will be fine. You're healthy. You'll get better."

"Sorry." He grimaced. "I keep telling myself to be patient, but I can't seem to remember."

"That's because you are not a particularly patient man," she said.

Lucas frowned slightly. "What do you mean?"

"Exactly what I said. You are not overly patient. You want things done at once."

"I sound like a pain to work for."

"I didn't say you were unreasonable about it. I just said that patience is not one of your strong points."

"But you love me, anyway?" he asked, wondering if his impatience was a source of conflict between them despite the fact that she sounded very casual about it.

A slight flush tinted her cheeks, but she forced herself to respond, "I love you, anyway."

Lucas felt something untwist in the region of his heart at her words. They sounded much too sincere to be faked. Not only that, but her flush added veracity to her words. Whatever else might be wrong in their relationship, he was sure she loved him. His spirits lifted.

"How about if we go buy our decorations after breakfast?" he said. "Then we can spend the afternoon hanging them."

"Sounds good to me." Jocelyn felt a happy warmth spread through her. Nothing he was suggesting was all that exciting. It was being able to do such homey things with the man she loved that made her feel so good. It was going to be a wonderful day.

# *Chapter Seven*

"Should I make a list?" Lucas asked as Jocelyn carefully backed the Mercedes out of the driveway.

"We already have a list. I'm your administrative assistant. Making lists is my job," she repeated absently, her attention focused on the small wren that was sitting at the end of the driveway. To her relief, as the car neared, it flew away.

Did he treat her like an employee even in their private life? he wondered uneasily.

"You may be my administrative assistant at work," he said. "But out of work you're my wife and, as far as I know, the only job description for a wife is to love her husband."

If only I really were his wife, Jocelyn thought on a wave of longing. Lucas would make a perfect husband. Kind and intelligent and a fantastic lover. A flush stained her cheeks as she remembered the kiss they'd shared.

Lucas watched the color wash over her pale cheeks in frustration. If only he knew what their relationship had been like before the accident. He felt as if he were groping around in the dark trying to fight an armed enemy who had perfect night vision. A faint stab of pain lanced through his left temple, and the very faintness of it helped to ease his frustration. Just yesterday his reaction to any strong emotion had been a sharp flash of pain that lingered. Today the pain was still there, but it was definitely muted.

He really was getting better, he realized. Everything Jocelyn had said was right. All he had to do was hang in there, and everything would be fine. He stole a glance at her face, his eyes lingering on the firmness of her tender mouth as she concentrated on driving over the light dusting of fresh snow that covered the narrow, winding road.

At least, physically everything would be fine. His emotional well-being seemed to be tied up in his wife. In some odd way, Jocelyn's presence made him feel complete. Whole. And when she smiled at him, he felt as if nothing was beyond him. As if no task was too difficult for him to accomplish.

Maybe his present emotional dependence on her was a result of the accident. He tried to analyze his reaction. They'd only been married for less than two months. He must have done all right before he'd known her.

Maybe, he conceded, but there was a whole lot of ground between doing all right and being happy, and he had the terrifying premonition that he'd never be happy again if Jocelyn wasn't there.

Don't borrow trouble, he thought, trying to pull himself out of his melancholy. If it's out there, it'll find you soon enough. You don't have to go looking for it.

"What is your job description for a husband?" he asked, hoping to get some insights into how she thought.

"What?" Jocelyn gave him a startled glance and then hurriedly refocused on the road.

"What do you want in a husband?" he persisted.

"You," she blurted out the truth.

Lucas felt his tension loosen at her reply.

"But you must have had some expectations for a husband."

Jocelyn frowned slightly, trying to sort out her feelings. "Not exactly. I mean, I never had a master list that I measured men by."

"Then, generally, what were you looking for in a husband? Money?" Lucas heard the question emerge from his mouth in surprise, wondering why he'd asked it.

"I'd be a hypocrite if I said that money wasn't important, because, speaking as someone who had to work her way through college, I can tell you the lack of it can be a real problem. But on the other hand, large sums of it aren't necessary to be happy. I want a husband who works at a job or, at least, is willing to work at one. Sometimes the most motivated person in the world can find himself out of work due to circumstances entirely beyond his control."

"True. Do you want to work?" he asked cautiously.

"Darn right I do," she said emphatically. "I spent seven years getting my degree, and I fully intend to use it."

"But what about children?" he asked. "Kids need a parent around."

"You're preaching to the converted," she said dryly. "I spent my childhood being shuffled from one foster home to another. But a child doesn't need a parent standing over him twenty-four hours a day. If both the husband and the wife are willing to work at it, they should be able to meet their children's needs."

"Why weren't you adopted?" he asked curiously. It really made no sense when he thought about it. She was a gorgeous woman so she must have been a really cute kid, and she was highly intelligent and very kind and caring, and those were traits that would certainly appeal to adoptive parents.

Jocelyn grimaced. "Because my mother refused to allow it. She kept insisting that she was going to clean up her act and bring me back home. And the social workers kept believing her."

Lucas felt a surge of anger at the bleakness of Jocelyn's expression. "What the hell did they think you were, a library book to be put on the shelf until your mother could pick you up again!"

Jocelyn sighed. "Sometimes it felt like that. It may not be fair, but kids are pretty much viewed as their parents' property. The whole focus of the social workers assigned to my case was to somehow turn my mother into a real mother. I was the bait that was supposed to do it, so they kept me in foster care."

Lucas's mind suddenly formed a picture of a blond, middle-aged woman with a discontented expression on her face. He blinked, and the image vanished.

"Was your mother a blonde?" he asked.

"No, she had brown hair. Why?"

"I just got a mental image of a blond woman and wondered if it was your mother."

"No, I've never shown you a picture of her."

"I wonder who the blonde was?" he said.

"At a guess, since we were talking about self-centered women, I'd say it was your stepmother. From the sound of her, she could have given my mother lessons."

"Where is my stepmother now?" Lucas asked curiously.

"Last I heard, she was on the French Riviera living with some Italian count."

"Do I support her?" Lucas asked.

"Nope, no need to. Your father left his entire fortune divided between your stepmother and your half brother. You got the company."

Lucas searched his emotions for a reaction to her words and came up empty. "I must have been happy with the division?" His voice rose questioningly.

"You never said otherwise," Jocelyn hedged.

"Have you met my half brother?"

"Bill is a loathsome rat!" she blurted out.

"I take it that means you've met him?" Lucas said dryly.

Jocelyn briefly weighed her options and, despite the fact that she didn't like the unexpected turn the conversation had taken, decided to give Lucas as much of the truth as she could.

"Yes, about a year before I met you. It was at a party given by your cousin Emmy."

"I have a cousin?"

"On your father's side. I think from the way Emmy explained it, she's actually a third cousin."

"And you say you met my half brother at a party my cousin gave?" Lucas persisted.

"Yes, a Christmas party. Emmy and I attended some college classes together."

"So what happened?" Lucas asked.

"Nothing much. Bill asked me out. I went. It didn't take long for me to figure out that the guy brought whole new shades of meaning to the term self-centered."

Lucas felt a surge of relief at her words. From the sound of things, she hadn't liked his half brother one little bit.

"I want—" He broke off, thrown against his seat belt,

as Jocelyn suddenly slammed on the brakes when a small, orangish animal darted in front of the car.

"Lucas, are you okay?" she asked anxiously.

"I'm fine," he said. "How about you?"

Jocelyn swallowed her stomach, which seemed to be lodged in her throat, and said, "I'm okay, but I'm worried about what I might have hit."

"A wild animal?" Lucas glanced up and down the deserted road and when he couldn't see any other cars coming, released his seat belt.

"Do wild animals come in orange? It…"

She broke off as a small, scruffy-looking dog came tearing out of the underbrush and disappeared beneath their car.

"What on earth?" She flipped on the car's flashers.

"Stay here while I check it out," he ordered.

"No, I was the one who…" She gulped at the thought of what the huge car might have done to a small animal. "I will be responsible for what happened."

Resolutely she climbed out and bent down to peer beneath the car, praying madly that she wouldn't see a bloody ball of squashed orange fur.

To her relief the orange fur was cowering beside the back right tire, and it appeared to be in one piece. The small dog was pressed against it as if he were trying to comfort it.

"It's a cat and a dog," she said uncertainly.

"In a manner of speaking," Lucas said dryly. Reaching beneath the car, he pulled out the cat and then scooped up the dog.

Jocelyn eyed the unprepossessing pair, and her heart twisted in pity as the dog began to shiver convulsively.

"The poor little things. They look half-starved," she said.

"They feel it, too," Lucas said grimly. "Get back into the car before someone comes along."

Jocelyn obediently got in, keeping a cautious eye on the road behind her as Lucas climbed in, the animals still in his arms.

"Let's go," Lucas said as the pair lay limply in his arms as if they didn't even have the energy to try to escape.

"But shouldn't we at least try to find out who they belong to?" she said uncertainly.

"I'd like to find out who let these animals get in this shape," Lucas's voice hardened, and the dog started to shiver.

"Sorry, boy." He calmed his voice. "Nothing personal.

"I would say these two were left to fend for themselves," he said. "Probably sometime last fall from the looks of them."

"Poor little things." Jocelyn obediently started forward, trying to figure out what she was going to do with them.

"We can't just take them to the pound," she finally said. "As undernourished as they look, they might not keep them. They might decide to..." She gulped at the thought. "Not only that, but I think they're friends, and the pound would probably separate them."

"No pound," Lucas agreed. "We passed an animal hospital when we were leaving the grocery store yesterday. Let's go there and see if the vet can look them over for us."

"Good idea." Jocelyn inadvertently sped up.

They had almost reached town when Lucas suddenly asked, "Do we have any pets?"

"Not so much as a goldfish," Jocelyn said.

"Do we like pets?"

"I like pets. How you feel about them never came up."

"I like these guys," Lucas said emphatically. "And they certainly deserve a break. Besides, the dog is a great watchdog. You saw how he came to his friend's rescue."

Jocelyn glanced at the shivering dog and grinned. "I think we'd better settle for making him an alarm dog. I don't think he's built for anything more physical."

Once Lucas regained his memory, she would take them home with her, she decided. Her apartment had no restrictions on pets, and they'd be company.

"We'll see." Lucas settled back, keeping a firm grip on the pair. He didn't want them to get free and startle Jocelyn and cause an accident.

They found the vet's office without any trouble. To Jocelyn's relief, the vet suggested they leave the pair at her office while they did their shopping and pick them up when they were finished. She said she would make time to look them over between her regularly scheduled appointments. She also confirmed Lucas's guess that they had probably been abandoned by some summer visitors who hadn't wanted to take them home.

"I can't believe that anyone would love a pet for an entire summer and then just drive off and leave them to fend for themselves," Jocelyn fumed as they drove away. "There ought to be a special place in hell for people like that."

"We can only hope. Let's try that big discount store at the edge of town," Lucas said. "We should be able to get everything we need for them in there."

"A conquering army could get everything they need in there, including firepower," she said tartly.

"You don't like it? We can go somewhere else."

"No, it's not that exactly. I simply abhor what these big megastores have done to the smaller retailers. Normally I would prefer to shop at one of them, even if it does cost a little more. But since I don't know where they are, and you don't remember, the discount store will do."

"Do I prefer small shops, too?" Lucas asked curiously as she adroitly parked the car.

"We never did any shopping together," she said.

Lucas considered her words as they walked across the parking lot. There seemed to be a lot of things they hadn't done together. What had they done with their time?

He studied the enticing pink of her cheeks out of the corner of his eye for a moment before his gaze slipped lower. Not even the bulky ski jacket she was wearing could disguise the perfection of her figure. He felt an answering spark of reaction from his body.

Was that the cause of the odd vibes he kept getting from her? Could they have married because of an overwhelming sexual attraction? And had she found, after the initial attraction had begun to wear off, that they didn't have a firm foundation of shared interests to build on? A surge of fear momentarily numbed his mind, but he refused to let it grow. If that were the case, and he didn't even know if it was, their time at the cabin would give him a chance to lay the foundation for their marriage. He already knew they shared an interest in work. And he knew she still desired him. Those were two big pluses.

He had plenty of tools. All he had to do was use them to build something lasting.

Lucas accepted a cart from the woman who pushed it to him as they entered the store. "Maybe each of us ought to take one." He eyed the cart consideringly.

"Let's start with one and see how that goes," Jocelyn said. "We're limited by the car's size as to how much we can bring home.

"Decorations first or pet supplies?" she asked,

Lucas looked at the floor map on the wall and said, "The decorations are closer according to this map. We'll start there."

"Lead on, Macduff."

"Right," Lucas said, knowing where he'd like to lead her. Straight to bed.

After a five-minute trek they found themselves in the midst of the biggest Christmas display she had ever seen.

"We should be able to find everything here," Lucas said.

Jocelyn eyed a two-foot-tall, animated Santa who was singing, "I Saw Mama Kissing Santa Claus." "Everything except good taste," she said ruefully.

Lucas steered the cart to the light display. "What kind of lights do we want to put up?"

"What about those?" She pointed to a display of icicle lights above their heads.

"They do kind of look like icicles. Do we want them in white or blue lights?"

"You choose," she offered.

"I think the blue ones," he finally said. Picking up a box, he studied it a minute and then placed it along with twelve more in the cart.

Jocelyn blinked, wondering where he was going to hang that many lights on the tiny lodge, but she held her peace. If it gave him pleasure, then it was fine by her.

"Look at that." He pointed to a multicolored ball, hanging from a hook at the end of the aisle.

"It looks like a disco ball in Christmas lights," Jocelyn said.

Lucas picked one up from the display and read the label on the box. "It says these can be hung outside."

"Like on a tree as ornaments?" She narrowed her eyes

trying to envision the results. Pretty spectacular, she rather imagined.

"Definitely," Lucas put five of them in the cart, eyed them for a moment and added another three.

"Do we need anything else here?" she asked.

"Extension cords," he said. "Outdoor ones. Then we can see about getting the pet stuff."

Jocelyn watched as Lucas added to the cart five extension cords and some kits for hanging lights up outside, and then she followed him out of the department.

"I want to pick up something in the pharmacy," she said. "How about if I meet you in the pet department?"

"No more medicine," he objected. "My headache is virtually a thing of the past."

"No more medicine," she agreed. "I was thinking more along the lines of antibiotic ointment and bandages for when you start putting all this stuff up."

He looked down his nose at her, his gorgeous eyes twinkling with good humor. "Oh, ye of little faith."

"Just think of me as the voice of experience," Jocelyn said. "Besides, if we're prepared for cuts and bruises, maybe we won't have any.

"I'll meet you in the pet department," she said as she hurried toward the pharmacy. It took her a matter of minutes to find the first-aid cream and bandages and then she added a pad that could be used either hot or cold for sprains and a large bottle of aspirin.

She hiked across the store to the pet department and arrived to find Lucas standing spellbound in the middle of an aisle.

Curious, she looked to see what he was studying so intently and found what appeared to be a six-foot-tall modern sculpture. A six-foot-tall, very bad modern sculpture.

''What is it?'' she asked curiously, poking at the carpet covering it.

''It's a cat perch,'' Lucas explained.

''They can't sit on the furniture like everyone else?''

''This gives them a place to climb and to scratch, and then when they're tired they can sleep on the perch,'' Lucas quoted from the display.

And it would totally fill one corner the lodge's small living room, she thought.

''But there wouldn't be anyplace on it for his dog friend,'' Jocelyn pointed out. ''And as close as they seem to be, I can't believe the cat would prefer to be by himself.''

''True,'' Lucas conceded. ''And there would be the problem of getting it home.''

Jocelyn giggled at the thought of trying to tie it to the car's roof. ''It certainly would present a challenge.''

Lucas felt his heart lift at her lighthearted laughter. Why was it that everything seemed so much more fun when she was around. As if her very presence brought vibrant color to a rather drab world.

''Maybe later,'' he finally said.

''Maybe,'' Jocelyn agreed.

Pulling out the list of essentials for animal care the vet's assistant has given them, Jocelyn began to load the supplies into the cart.

''What about coats?'' Lucas asked, gesturing to a display to his right.

Jocelyn studied the racks of brightly colored sweaters and finally said, ''Makes sense to me. I wouldn't want to wander around outside in this weather without something on. Let's get the dog several because I'll bet they get wet quickly.''

Lucas obediently picked out three sweaters and tossed them into the overflowing cart.

"Do we need anything else?" he asked.

"I don't think so. The vet said we could get animal carriers and food from her. And we got everything else on the list."

"Then let's check out and go home," Lucas said.

*Home,* the word sounded so very sweet to Jocelyn.

# *Chapter Eight*

"What kind of cars do we normally drive?" Lucas asked Jocelyn.

She finished squeezing the animal supplies they'd gotten from the vet into the car, closed it and came around to where Lucas was fastening the animals' carriers into the back seat.

"Cars?" she repeated, wondering what had prompted the question.

"Surely you have your own car?" He yanked on the seat belt holding the dog's carrier in place to make sure it was secure, closed the door and got into the front seat.

Jocelyn slipped behind the wheel and then said, "I drive a compact and you drive a Mercedes S class."

Lucas frowned. "I drive a Mercedes, and you make do with a compact?"

"I happen to like my car. It's easy to drive, easy to park and doesn't use much gas."

"Maybe, but I was thinking that we ought to get one of those." He gestured to the minivan parked beside them.

"Why?" Jocelyn asked as she carefully pulled out into the road.

"Because all we have at the moment is two small pets, and this car is already full. What will happen when we have a kid? We need more room."

Jocelyn felt a warmth spark to life deep within her at his casual mention of them having children. Hastily she tamped it down, forcing herself to face reality. Buying a few Christmas decorations was one thing, letting him buy a car was something else again. There would be no way to justify the expense once he regained his memory.

"I think we'd better wait until we have a kid before we start worrying about transporting it," she finally said.

She decided to change the subject to something less emotionally fraught than the thought of having his children. "What about names?"

"I like Sophia if it's a girl and Robert if it's a boy. Of course, what I'll like when I get my mind back is anybody's guess," he added wryly.

"You haven't lost your mind, just temporarily misplaced your memory, and I wasn't talking about kids' names. I meant for the pair in the back seat."

Lucas turned and glanced over his shoulder, wincing at the way the two animals were cowering in their carriers.

"Poor little devils," he said. "They look as if it's ten minutes after the end of the world. Maybe I should have gotten the cat that climbing thing, after all."

"They'll perk up once we start feeding them on a regular basis. But we can't keep calling them the animals."

"No," Lucas agreed. "Do you have any ideas?"

"Well, the dog seems to be some kind of terrier mix. He can't weigh more than ten pounds and the vet thought he was full-grown." She thought a moment and said, "He looks like a Percy."

"Percy? What does a Percy look like?"

"Victorian, to me at least. I think it's his side whiskers. The Victorians used to go in for lots of facial hair."

"Percy it is," Lucas agreed. "What about the cat?"

"Something short, maybe...Max?" she suggested. "Prince Albert was definitely Victorian, and he was German, and Max is a German name so they match."

Lucas grinned at her. "Have I ever told you you have the most incredibly convoluted thought processes?"

"Thank you." She grinned back. "Convoluted thought is a big plus in the business world. We..."

Jocelyn broke off as she caught sight of a dark-haired man coming out of the restaurant they were passing. She tried to get a better look without being obvious about it, but she couldn't. The man had turned slightly to study the headlines in the newspaper-vending machine beside the door.

Jocelyn swallowed deliberately, trying to force down the sudden uprush of fear she'd felt. It couldn't have been Bill, she told herself. He didn't know they were in Vermont. Did he?

Nervously she caught her lower lip between her teeth and tried to think. The only person she had told was Richard, and Richard wouldn't give Bill the time of day. Not only did Richard dislike Bill personally, but Richard knew how Lucas felt about his half brother. Both loyalty and common sense would dictate that Richard not betray his boss.

But Lucas had owned the lodge for years. Bill had to know about it.

You don't know that it was Bill, she tried to tell herself. You only got a glimpse of him out of the corner of your eye. You only think it's him because he's preying on your mind.

"Is anything the matter?" Lucas asked. "Are you sure you don't want me to drive?"

Jocelyn made a determined effort to shake off her fears. Worrying about Bill wasn't going to make him go away.

"Believe me, I'm sure I don't want you to drive, and nothing is the matter. I was just thinking."

"Well, try thinking about something a little more cheerful," he said. "You looked like you had a touch of what was affecting Percy and Max."

Lucas was certainly right about that, Jocelyn thought. She and Percy and Max were all suffering from the lack of an emotional anchor in their lives.

She'd call Bill when she got back and see if he was home, she decided. If he was, then she'd know he couldn't have been in town. And if he wasn't... That still didn't mean it had been him, she told herself. Just because he wasn't in his apartment didn't mean that he was here in Vermont.

"Maybe you ought to lie down for a while when we get back," Lucas said.

"No, I'm fine. Besides, I want to get those decorations up this afternoon. It gets dark so early."

"If you're sure. How about if we'll settle the animals first, then put up the decorations, then light a fire and toast marshmallows and hot dogs."

Jocelyn shuddered. "I don't even want to think about what all this fast food is doing to your cholesterol level."

"Do I have a problem?"

"Not that I know of."

"Then a few odd meals won't hurt anything," he said.

"True. But tomorrow we're going to cook a real meal, completely with all the basic food groups."

"Are you trying to tell me that chocolate isn't one of the basic food groups?"

Jocelyn chuckled. ''Dream on.''

''Please leave me with a few illusions.''

Jocelyn bit her lip. Lucas wasn't going to have any illusions left at all once he found out about her impersonation. But she was doing it for his own good, she reminded herself. She just hoped he would see it that way. At least eventually. Remembering how coldly furious he had been when she'd handed in her notice, she had no doubt what his initial reaction would be.

Twenty-five minutes later, Jocelyn pulled into their driveway, parking the car in front of the house to make it easier to unpack.

''You take Percy and Max inside, and I'll unpack the car,'' Lucas said. ''Where do you want me to put things?''

''Just set everything in the living room, and we can sort it all out later,'' she said as she switched off the engine.

Getting out of the car, she opened the back door and unfastened the seat belt around Percy's carrier. The little dog gave her a look in which cautious hope and abject fear were equally mixed.

''It's all right, Percy,'' she said soothingly. ''You're going to be just fine. You've got someone to belong to now, and we'll take very good care of you.''

She pulled his carrier out of the car, being careful not to jar it.

''I've unlocked the door,'' Lucas said around the armful of bags he was holding. ''Leave him in the carrier until I can locate that leash we bought, and I'll give him a quick walk.''

''I wonder if the vet is right and he's already housebroken?'' Jocelyn said as she followed Lucas into the house.

''It would make sense if he's someone's pet, but even

if he isn't, we can train him easily enough. He looks like a smart little beast."

"That he does," Jocelyn agreed. "Brave, too, to have run under the car to try to rescue his friend."

"You sit there, Percy, while I go get Max," Jocelyn told the shivering dog.

She hurried back to the car and quickly brought in the cat carrier, setting it down facing Percy so the two could see each other. Percy strained against the wire mesh in the front of his carrier trying to reach his friend.

"Just give us a minute, boy," Jocelyn said. "First a walk for you, and then I'll set up Max's litter box and then you two can be free."

"I found them." Lucas held up the bright red leash and matching collar they'd bought.

Jocelyn carefully unlatched the carrier's door and gently scooped up the cowering dog. "It's okay, handsome," she murmured. "Nobody's going to hurt you."

Lucas quickly fastened the collar around Percy's neck, attached the leash and gently took the animal out of Jocelyn's arms.

"Just a quick walk and then we'll come right back inside. I promise," Lucas told him.

Percy responded by giving Lucas a furtive lick on the chin.

"I think he likes me." Lucas sounded both surprised and pleased.

"Why shouldn't he?" Jocelyn said. "You're a very likable man."

Lucas leaned over and dropped a quick kiss on her month. "Thank you, but then I would expect you to say that. We are married, after all."

"From what I've seen, marriage is no guarantee that couples will like each other," she said dryly.

"Then we must be the exception that proves the rule," Lucas said, "because I not only like you, I love you. Lust after you, too, for all the good it does me." His voice took on a plaintive note.

"Next month." Jocelyn forced the words out past her overwhelming sense of guilt.

"Next month," he repeated as he picked up the dog and headed toward the door.

While Lucas walked Percy, Jocelyn hurriedly set up the cat's litter box. Then she gently pulled Max out of his carrier and showed it to him. He promptly darted into it, used it and then emerged to study her nervously.

"What a clever little cat you are," Jocelyn praised him. "You want to help me decide where we should put your beds?"

Encouraged by the fact that he didn't try to run from her, Jocelyn took the steel dog bed and the cloth cat bed, which was shaped like an igloo, and looked around the room.

"Not too close to the fireplace," she murmured to Max. "I don't want you getting hit with a stray spark. And not against an outside wall 'cause that's bound to be colder. How about over here?" She placed the beds on the wall between the living room and the kitchen.

"You can try out your new bed," Jocelyn told the cat. "Or not, as the case may be," she added when Max continued to watch her with an unwavering stare.

She turned as the door opened and Lucas reappeared, holding Percy.

"I wonder if they sell boots for dogs?" he asked.

"They sell those fancy rhinestone collars, so they probably do. Why do you want to get him boots?"

"Because his feet get all wet in the snow. Can you got something to wipe them with?"

Jocelyn hurried into the bathroom to get a hand towel and carefully dried off Percy's feet. "I think he's going to have problems when it snows again," she said. "He's built rather low to the ground."

"I'll shovel him out a spot," Lucas promised, carefully setting the dog down in his dog bed.

Percy immediately jumped out of the bed and raced over to the cat. He sniffed Max as if reassuring himself that his friend was all right, and then the pair of them hurried over to Percy's bed and climbed in.

"I guess they're used to being together," Lucas said.

"Probably. Once they feel a little more at home, Max will use his own bed."

"Why don't I get them something to eat while you unpack the lights?"

She paused halfway to the kitchen. "I wonder if we have a stepladder?"

"If we don't, we can use a kitchen chair. It's probably high enough."

"A kitchen chair!" Jocelyn gave him a scandalized look. "Those chairs are solid maple."

"So? The maple tree they came from must have spent years outside in all kinds of weather."

"Yes, but..."

"No buts, the lights go up today, even if we have to use a kitchen chair."

"Okay," Jocelyn agreed, reminding herself that it was his chair. And if he didn't care that it did double duty as a footstool, why should she?

"I'll go check the garage to see what's out there in the line of equipment," Lucas said.

"I'll be out in a minute," Jocelyn said, intending to check the phone messages at her apartment while he was outside.

Lucas gathered up the bags with the icicle lights and hurried out the front door. The anticipation on his face made her heart twist with tenderness.

She quickly fed the animals and then pulled her cell phone out of her purse and quickly dialed her apartment number. The first message was from Bill. She swallowed and forced herself to listen to the words and not to the annoying manner in which the message had been delivered.

What on earth was he talking about? she wondered as she hit the replay button. The machine obligingly repeated the message.

"Hey, babe, that was positively inspired of you to get old Lucas out of the way like you did. I'm going to search his apartment for the missing will. Just make sure you keep him there until after ten tonight. We wouldn't want him to come back and find me here and realize why you were so keen to get him up to Vermont, now would we?" Bill ended the message with a laugh that was an obscene parody of good humor.

There was absolutely no mistaking the threat in Bill's words. Cooperate or else.

Jocelyn turned off the cell phone, replaced it in her purse and then sank down on the couch as she tried to think.

Bill was going to search Lucas's apartment this evening while Lucas was safely out of the way here at the lodge. And in order to search Lucas's apartment he would first have to break into it, because Lucas would never have given him a key.

And if Bill were breaking into Lucas's apartment that meant that he was also breaking the law. She chewed her lower lip. She didn't know if it was breaking and entering or burglary or something else but it was definitely illegal.

What would happen if she were to call the police and tell them she suspected someone was going to burglarize Lucas's apartment while he was away? The police would undoubtedly stake out the apartment and catch Bill red-handed.

Her spirits soared at the thought and then plummeted when she thought about what would happen next.

Bill would undoubtedly claim that he was Lucas's half brother and had a right to be there. The police would call Lucas to verify the fact. And then what would happen? Lucas wouldn't remember his half brother. Even if Lucas asked her what to do and she urged him to press charges, Bill would never keep quiet. Not only would he tell Lucas all sorts of lies about their supposed affair last year, but Lucas would be certain to find out that they weren't married. And there was no telling how that revelation would affect him physically or mentally. No, confronting Bill was a bad idea.

What would happen if she did nothing about Bill's message? She considered the alternative. If she just allowed him to search Lucas's apartment?

Probably nothing, she finally decided. Since there wasn't any will for Bill to find, he couldn't find it. Nor would Bill find anything else that could cause problems. Lucas was scrupulously honest. She was sure there was nothing he did either personally or professionally that needed to be hidden away from public view.

Jocelyn grimaced in frustration. Much as she hated to let Bill get away with it, she didn't have any choice. Stopping him would cause far more damage than letting him go ahead.

There was one good thing, though. That man she'd caught a glimpse of in town hadn't been Bill. He might have somehow managed to find out where they were, but Bill himself was still in Philadelphia.

"Hey." Lucas stuck his head inside the front door, "Come on, Jocelyn. I found a six-foot stepladder in the garage. Let's go."

"Coming." Jocelyn jumped to her feet only too glad to stop brooding about how she always seemed to come out on the losing end whenever she tangled with Bill.

She slipped back into her parka, jammed her wool cap down over her ears and then noticed the animals who were watching her every move.

"You two be good." She gently rubbed the top of Percy's head and stroked Max's back. "If you need us, just give a yowl and we'll come running."

Max ignored her, but Percy gave a tentative thump of his tail.

Grabbing her leather gloves, she hurried outside after Lucas.

He had set the ladder up at one end of the house and was waiting beside it with a string of icicle lights in his hand.

"I'll hang lights. You hold the ladder," she told him.

"There is no reason I can't just stand on the bottom rung to put them up," he argued. "This house isn't very tall."

"A fall is a fall is a fall," she repeated stubbornly.

"And a fanatic is a fanatic is a fanatic," he grumbled.

"I'm not strong enough to catch you if the ladder should suddenly slip on the snow, whereas you can catch me," she said, trying logic.

"Hmm." Lucas eyed her with a devilish spark in his eye. "Maybe and maybe not," he said slowly.

Jocelyn stared uncomprehendingly at him. "Maybe what?"

"Don't forget, I'm in a weakened condition," he said. "Have you taken that into consideration?"

He wasn't weakened in any way that mattered to her, she thought, swallowing to relieve the sudden dryness in her mouth as he moved closer, stopping scant inches in front of her.

"We should be sure."

"Oh, definitely," she muttered, having no idea what he was talking about and not really caring. She was too caught up with the excitement of being so close to him, with breathing in the heady aroma of his cologne which was mixed with the chill crispness of the afternoon air.

She let out a surprised squeak when he suddenly swooped and lifted her in his arms.

"What are you doing?" she blurted out.

"Making sure I really can rescue you." His voice was serious, but his eyes were gleaming with suppressed laughter.

And who was going to rescue her from him? she wondered. Certainly not her own common sense, which wasn't even making a token protest.

"What do you think?" Lucas asked. "Am I up to the job?"

"I'll say," she muttered, and froze as his mouth swooped downward to plant a kiss on her lips. His arms tightened, binding her closer to him. Instinctively she clutched his neck and pressed herself closer still, her lips parting.

His tongue was quick to take advantage of her invitation, and he began a leisurely exploration of the inside of her mouth.

A slow, burning warmth washed through her, sending a hectic flush over her cheeks.

He dropped a last kiss on the tip of her reddened nose

and gently let her slide down the length of his body till her feet touched the snow-covered ground.

Jocelyn locked her knees to support her trembling limbs. She found it absolutely amazing that this man's kiss could be so different from all the other men she'd kissed in her life. But then, Lucas was the only man she'd ever been in love with. It really did make a difference when you were in love. And it was going to make a big difference in her life when he was no longer there, she thought grimly.

"Why so solemn?" Lucas asked her uncertainly.

"I'm cold. We'd better get on with this so we can finish before dark. Or before one of us freezes to death, whichever comes first," she said.

"Right." Lucas reached into his pocket and pulled out a packet of white plastic clips. "The directions say to hook these over the eaves and then hang the lights on them."

Jocelyn studied the hooks for a long minute, looked up at the eaves and then back down at the lights. "I can handle that," she said.

Ripping the package open, she scrambled up the ladder, attached the hooks and then the lights. Rather to her surprise, not only was it relatively effortless, but it was quick. With Lucas's help, she completely outlined the small house in an hour and a half.

It was the work of another half hour to hang all eight of the colored disco-ball lights on the two trees in the front yard.

Jocelyn picked up the empty boxes and carried them into the garage for storage while Lucas plugged the extension cords into the outside outlets.

"Ready for the official lighting?" he asked when she returned to the front of the house.

"Ready," she replied. "Give it your best shot, Edison."

Lucas obediently plugged in the cords.

"Good heavens!" she gasped, momentarily dazzled by the brilliance of the colored balls hanging in the trees. "They're gorgeous!"

"It is rather nice, isn't it?" Lucas studied the house. "Do you think we need more lights?"

Jocelyn eyed it critically. "No, besides everyone is going to be so taken up with those colored balls they aren't going to notice the house. Lit up they remind me even more of a disco."

Lucas picked up the ladder and started around the house toward the garage. Jocelyn followed along behind him.

"Did we go to discos very often?" he asked, trying to remember dancing with Jocelyn in his arms and failing.

"I haven't been to a disco since my early twenties and never with you. The noise and the confusion lost its appeal very quickly," she said.

Jocelyn held the garage door for him while he replaced the ladder where he had found it.

"What kinds of things do we do for fun?" Lucas asked her.

Jocelyn hastily searched her memory and came up with a couple of things they had done together when they had been on business trips.

"Oh, the normal," she said. "We both like concerts and dining out and used-book stores, and you are very fond of medieval armor."

Lucas had a brief flash of a glass case filled with silver suits of armor. "I am?"

"I'll say. We spent one whole afternoon at the Met the last time we were in New York studying their armor collection."

"I take it you don't like armor?" he asked, wondering if he was the kind of person who expected his wife to cater to his interests and ignored hers.

"Actually I found it rather interesting," she said. "And impressive. Those guys must have had muscles on their muscles to have carried all that weight around. And you promised to take me to a Renaissance fair the next time one was in the Philadelphia area so I could see what else went on in the Middle Ages besides fighting."

"I will," he vowed, determined to convince her that her interests were important to him.

Lucas swept a look around the deck across the back of the house as he opened the kitchen door. "It looks pretty bare back here. Maybe we ought to light it up some?"

"Couldn't hurt. How about if we get some more of those balls and hang then from the bottom limbs of that tree." She pointed to a small maple in the backyard. "We could see them out the patio door from the living room."

"Good idea," Lucas approved. "We'll get some more tomorrow before someone buys them all."

Jocelyn chuckled. "You mean before someone *else* buys them all."

He grinned back. "Semantics. Why don't I take Percy out again while you build a fire. Then we can roast hot dogs and toast marshmallows."

"It's a deal," she agreed.

Jocelyn quickly got a fire burning. Replacing the fire screen, she looked up to see Max pressed up against the patio doors watching Percy.

"He'll be back in a few minutes," she said, dropping to her knees beside the obviously worried cat. "You're safe now, Max. I won't let anything happen to the pair of you."

She gently stroked her hand over his back. "How about

a little more food, boy? That vet said you should have a small amount at frequent intervals until you've recovered from being half-starved.''

Max ignored her, his entire focus on keeping Percy in sight.

Getting to her feet, she went out into the kitchen and measured out a few spoonfuls of food for each animal and then carried the bowls back into the living room and set them down besides Max.

She would gradually move their food back into the kitchen once they felt more at home, she decided. Right now they clearly didn't feel secure enough to go looking for their meals.

Max apparently didn't feel secure enough to even turn his head and eat without Percy there, since he ignored his food until Lucas returned with his friend.

Once Percy was let off his leash, the dog dashed into the living room, sniffed Max and then inhaled his dinner.

Max sidled up to his tuna fish and daintily gulped it down.

''I'm with Percy,'' Lucas said. ''Starved.''

''Why don't you find those toasting forks we bought, and I'll get the food. The fire's going well enough.''

''Okay,'' he said. ''Then after dinner we can snuggle up and...''

He looked around the living room as if he were searching for something.

''What's wrong?'' she asked.

''We don't seem to have a CD player. Or a television, or even a radio. I wonder why?''

''Maybe you didn't like distractions from your skiing?'' she guessed.

''Seems to me that a skier, particularly one who is commuting, would want immediate access to the weather. And some music would be very soothing in the evenings,'' he said. ''We'll get a CD player, a selection of CDs, a radio and a television tomorrow when we pick up the rest of the balls for the backyard.''

Jocelyn blinked at the amount of money he was spending. He might not be too happy about it once he regained his memory. But then, there were so many other things he was going to be furious about when he regained his memory that money wasn't going to be very high up his list. Besides which, Lucas had never been a stingy man. Not professionally and not personally.

She just hoped he didn't turn out to be a vengeful man or she was in deep trouble, she thought uneasily.

# *Chapter Nine*

The vaguely threatening sound of something snuffling at the bedroom door penetrated Lucas's sleep, and his eyelids twitched as his groggy mind struggled to identify it.

Percy, he finally realized. The dog was trying to find out where he was. Well, Percy could wait another half hour to satisfy his curiosity, Lucas thought drowsily. He snuggled deeper into his warm bed and bumped up against the yielding body beside him.

His eyes shot open in surprise, and he found himself staring into Jocelyn's sleep-relaxed face. His entire body tensed at the intoxicating sight. She was so gorgeous, he thought, as he hungrily studied her soft, slightly parted lips. If he were to lean forward just a little, he could brush his lips against hers and…

Jocelyn? He gasped as a feeling of vertigo swept over him, giving him the disconcerting feeling that he was falling. He froze as his memory came rushing back in a confusing tidal wave of jumbled events, emotions and totally unrelated trivia. He pressed his lips together to hold back his rising nausea. After a few interminable minutes, the sensation of not being in control of his own thoughts passed, and he tried to make sense of what had happened.

The accident. That was the place to start. He'd had an accident. He winced as his mind obligingly supplied an image of a large black car skidding toward him. Lucas frowned, trying to remember what had happened immediately after that, but he couldn't. All he could remember was a car as big as a mountain coming toward him. The next memory he was able to come up with was of Jocelyn's white face leaning over him. She had looked frightened and intent, but why she was frightened and what she seemed so set on he didn't know. Nor could he be positive that he actually had seen her. Maybe he was simply imagining it.

Hadn't he read somewhere that traumatic events played tricks on one's memory? And things didn't get much more traumatic than being mowed down by a car.

As Jocelyn muttered and shifted slightly in her sleep, he tensed, not wanting her to wake up. He desperately wanted to get everything straight in his mind before he had to face her.

To his relief she simply snuggled a little closer to him and continued to sleep.

Determined to figure out what was going on, Lucas forced his mind back to the accident and carefully traced what he could remember. But instead of clearing up his confusion, what he remembered simply increased it. Jocelyn must have claimed to have been his wife at the scene of the accident, since the hospital believed it. But why had she done it? He couldn't come up with a single good reason. She'd already given her notice. She was due to leave in…

He tried to remember what day it was, but he couldn't.

The time around his accident was too confused. He wasn't sure how many days he'd lost. But even so, his accident would have released her from working out the rest of her notice. She could have left him in the hospital and flown home on her original ticket. But she hadn't done that. Why not was the question? What could she hope to gain by pretending to be his wife?

Plenty, he thought, as an image of his stepmother's sharp features filled his mind. If he thought Jocelyn was his wife then he would have allowed her access to his bank accounts. And they were substantial.

But she hadn't drained any of his accounts, he conceded as he mentally reviewed the last few days. All they had bought was a bunch of Christmas decorations and that had been his idea.

Jocelyn wasn't stupid. She had to know that any financial gains she expected to make would have to be done quickly because that doctor had been very specific about his memory returning at any time.

And there was a second problem with that theory, he realized. When she'd originally claimed to be his wife, she couldn't have known that he was going to lose his memory. So why make the claim in the first place?

Unless... Could she feel something for him? A sudden jolt of excitement slammed through him, before his common sense doused the idea. If Jocelyn felt anything for him, she wouldn't have quit. And she had. Very forcefully.

He felt like throwing something. Something heavy. None of this made any sense. Especially not her sudden resignation, when just the week before they'd been making plans about what they were going to do with the company in the spring.

Although it did make sense if she had taken the job as

his administrative assistant with the intention of trapping him into a relationship as his stepmother had done with his father...and had then resigned when she'd believed she wasn't making any progress. She should have waited a few more weeks, he thought with a sour taste in his mouth. A little more patience on her part, and she would have been rewarded by seeing him make a monumental fool of himself.

But even if all that was true, and even if she had claimed to be his wife to try to take financial advantage of him, the fact still remained that she hadn't. And he hadn't a clue as to why not.

Jocelyn moved slightly, and he tensed. He had to figure out what he was going to do about the bizarre situation he found himself in, and he had to do it fast.

Basically he had two options, he decided. He could tell her he'd regained his memory, or he could continue to pretend to have amnesia. If he told her he had his memory back, then it was over. He'd never know why she had begun the pretense in the first place. He would always be left wondering if she was simply another predatory woman like his stepmother, who used her sensuality as a trap, or if there was more to her impersonation than that. And he wanted to know. Needed to know. All he had to do was to play dumb a little longer. Give her a little more time to make her move, and then he'd know. For sure. He wouldn't have to guess.

He couldn't keep the pretense up indefinitely because he had a company to run, but he could manage it until after Christmas, he finally decided. And, if nothing else, it would give him memories of one holiday spent with the woman he loved.

Lucas went rigid as he realized the word his subconscious had used. He didn't "love" her, he told himself, fighting a rearguard action against his emotions. Loving Jocelyn would be a disaster. She would just leave him. Hell, she was already planning on leaving him.

A whining noise suddenly cut through his circular thoughts. Percy had given up on the subtle approach and was now trying a more direct one. The poor beast probably needed to go outside.

Cautiously Lucas eased himself out of bed. He hurriedly dressed and quietly slipped out the door to find Percy lying just outside it. Max was pressed up against him.

The dog gave him a pathetically hopeful look as if praying for friendliness but prepared to be abused.

Lucas bent over and gently scratched behind his ears, then lightly stroked Max.

"Morning, guys. Give me five minutes to get my shoes on and find my coat and I'll take you out, Percy."

Max ignored him, but Percy thumped his raggedy tail on the carpet.

Lucas hurried and three minutes later slipped outside the patio doors with the dog. Percy wasted no time. It was as if he was afraid that if he stayed outside too long, Lucas might decide to leave him there.

"How about breakfast?" Lucas asked once they were back inside.

Percy gave him an encouraging whine, and Lucas went into the kitchen and ladled out the small portions the vet had recommended. Percy gulped down his food and then looked at Lucas clearly asking for more.

"Sorry, boy. I'll give you some more in an hour."

Percy cocked one ear, turned his head to one side as if listening and hurried into the living room. Max continued to eat his breakfast with dainty bites.

Lucas went to see what had interested the dog and

found Jocelyn standing just in the bedroom petting Percy. Hungrily, his eyes traced over her slight figure. She was wearing a pair of jeans that lovingly molded her legs and a thick cream-colored sweater. She looked good enough to eat. As far as he was concerned the only way she would look better would be if she were wearing a lacy negligee. A green one, he decided, made of a soft supple silk that would cling to her curves. He ran the tip of his tongue over his suddenly dry lips as his mind painted a picture of her breasts almost covered by the lacy décolletage. He'd…

"Is your head bothering you?" Her prosaic question yanked him out of his delightful speculation.

Careful, Forester, don't let her suspect anything is different this morning or it's all over. She'll take off like a rabbit, and you'll never have any answers.

"No, just a little cold. Percy and I were outside."

Jocelyn quickly looked around the living room. "Any accidents?"

"Not a one. Our Percy was clearly someone's pet before he became someone's castoff."

Our Percy. Jocelyn savored the phrase. As if they were a team. And for the moment it was true. For as long as Lucas's memory stayed in limbo they were a team.

Percy licked her hand, and she smiled down at the little beast. A team that was growing by the day.

She looked up to find Lucas staring at her with an intense expression on his face. She recognized the look. It was one he wore when he was perplexed by something and determined to get to the bottom of it.

Could he have regained his memory? A sudden feeling of dread iced her skin. She was imagining things, she assured herself. If he'd regained his memory, he would be demanding to know was what was going on. And he wasn't. He hadn't even made any oblique references to the situation.

"I've fed them," Lucas said. "How about if we plan our day while we eat?"

Jocelyn relaxed at his words as she followed him out to the kitchen.

"How about some oatmeal?" she said as she got the box of cereal out of the cabinet.

Lucas eyed the small packet she was emptying into a bowl.

"Better make that two for me," he said. "Have we got any doughnuts to snack on while we wait?"

"You're only waiting ninety seconds," she said dryly. "And doughnuts are bad for you. They clog up your arteries."

"Doughnuts are food for the soul," Lucas announced. "Haven't you ever heard of feeding one's inner self?"

"Sure I have, along with high blood pressure, high cholesterol and..."

"It's too early in the morning to dwell on the gruesome details," Lucas said.

"Moot, too," she said, "since we don't have any doughnuts. Make do with your oatmeal."

Jocelyn set the steaming bowl in front of him.

Lucas added some milk and started eating with a sense of satisfaction. He'd done it! She hadn't realized that he had his memory back. Now all he had to do was to keep it up. That and figure out how to get her to tip her hand. But how could he do that? he wondered as he absently worked his way through his cereal.

"Don't look so sad," Jocelyn said. "If you really want doughnuts, we can get you some while we're in town."

"We'll stop at the bakery," he absently agreed.

Jocelyn felt a sudden frisson of unease at his words.

''What bakery? Did you remember something?''

Lucas cursed his careless words. This was going to be harder than he'd thought.

''No,'' he lied. ''The waitress at the restaurant mentioned that that was where their pies came from. It was while you were getting that prescription filled.'' And making that phone call you didn't want me to know about, he remembered.

''Oh.'' Jocelyn relaxed at his explanation.

''So what are we going to do today?'' she asked, once they had finished their oatmeal.

''We're going back into town. We'll find a place that sells electronics and get a CD player, a television and anything else that appeals to us. Anything you particularly want?'' Lucas watched her closely to see if she took advantage of his offer to buy her something.

To his surprise, she ignored his offer.

''Maybe we should rent all that stuff,'' Jocelyn said. ''It seems like a lot of expense and, if you'd wanted them in the first place surely you would have already bought them?''

''Do we have any financial problems you've been keeping from me?'' Lucas asked, curious as to what she would say.

''I meant it when I told you that you can afford to buy anything you want, but that doesn't mean you're going to approve of having spent a lot of money once you regain your memory.''

''*I* can afford? Tell me, since I can't remember the wedding ceremony, have they changed it?'' Lucas couldn't resist pushing.

''Doesn't it go something along the lines of 'with all my worldly goods I thee endow'?'' he quoted a line from a wedding he'd attended recently.

Jocelyn frowned, "How did you know that?"

"Oh, I know lots of facts. It's remembering personal facts that gives me trouble," he said.

"The justice of the peace who married us might have said that, but I was too nervous to remember."

"He probably did," Lucas said. "I can't imagine a justice of the peace getting original about a wedding ceremony. Maybe we ought to get remarried right now, so I can at least remember that ceremony?"

Lucas watched her narrowly to see how she reacted.

"No!" Jocelyn blurted out, ruthlessly suppressing the sense of longing that flooded her at his unexpected words. "We can get remarried again once you regain your memory," she said, to soften her refusal.

Lucas winced at the uncompromising tone of her rejection. Clearly she didn't want to marry him, so what the hell did she want? He gritted his teeth against an urge to ask her and struggled for a light tone.

"Tell you what, since you're worried about me spending my money, how about we spend the half of my money that I bequeathed to you?" he finally said.

"You sound like a Philadelphia lawyer, not a businessman," she said.

"Please, no insults so early in the morning. Do you remember what time the stores open?"

"The grocery store is open twenty-four hours as is the discount store. Most everything else should be open by ten. That's a pretty standard time."

Lucas checked his watch. "Okay. Let's hit the discount store for more of those Christmas balls and some more extension cords, then we can see about the other stuff."

"Okay," Jocelyn agreed, feeling faintly uneasy. For a moment Lucas had sounded exactly like Lucas had sounded before his accident. Decisive and focused.

Uncertainly she stared at him. Maybe it was simply that with each passing day he was becoming more and more himself? It made sense. At least, it made as much sense as anything in this whole mess did.

Maybe she could… She lost her train of thought as she suddenly heard her cell phone ringing.

''What's that?'' Lucas turned and stared out into the living room where she had left the phone sitting on an end table.

''My cell phone.'' She hurriedly got to her feet. ''It's probably just a friend. That or Richard calling with an update on the business.''

She hurried into the living room, grabbed the phone and answered it. To her dismay, it was neither a girlfriend nor Richard. It was Bill's voice that scraped irritatingly across her nerves.

''The dammed will wasn't there!'' Bill immediately launched into a complaint. ''I took his apartment apart piece by piece, and it wasn't there. It must be at the lodge, I tell you.''

There were a lot of things Jocelyn wanted to say, starting with she wished he wouldn't tell her anything ever again and ending with she wanted him to disappear down a deep dark hole. But she couldn't for several reasons—not the least of which was the fact that Lucas was standing behind her listening to everything she said. He might have lost his memory, but there was nothing wrong with his wits. She absolutely couldn't say anything to make him suspicious. A little investigation on Lucas's part and her impersonation would collapse around her.

''Answer me, dammit!'' Bill yelled.

''I didn't realize you'd asked a question.'' Jocelyn kept her voice level with a monumental effort.

"Don't act any dumber than I already know you are! It has to be at the lodge."

"It isn't," she insisted.

"And how would you know?"

"I looked," she lied.

"You probably weren't looking in the right places. Get Lucas out of there, and I'll do the job right. I flew up last night after I realized he had to have stashed the will at the lodge. I can be at his place in half an hour."

Jocelyn's heart sank at the appalling information. The very thought of Bill pawing through her belongings made her skin crawl. Not only that, but Lucas would be bound to notice if the lodge was searched, and he would call the police, and who knew what might come to light if they got involved. Somehow she had to stall Bill long enough to...

An idea occurred to her as her gaze landed on the two animals huddled in Percy's bed.

"Have I mentioned that Lucas has acquired a dog?" she said.

"A dog!" Bill repeated incredulously. "What the hell would he want with a dog?"

"It needed a home. It's really a cute animal other than the fact that it doesn't seem to be very trusting, but I hope that once it feels secure it won't be quite so..." She purposefully let her voice trail away suggestively.

"What kind of dog is it?" Bill asked suspiciously.

"Oh, you know, just a dog. The vet thinks he has a fair amount of pit bull in him, but I'm sure she's wrong about the aggressive tendency." Jocelyn sent an apologetic smile at poor Percy. "I mean mostly he just sits there and watches you. That and wolf down his food. I think he was starved."

"You stupid bitch," Bill sputtered. "Starving an animal is one of the ways they train them to fight. That damn thing sounds dangerous.''

''I doubt it,'' Jocelyn said, well satisfied with his reaction. With any luck at all, he would be too frightened of being bitten to try breaking into the lodge.

''You've got to get rid of it,'' Bill demanded.

''It isn't mine to do anything with. I will, however, go over things one more time,'' she hurriedly added, hoping that the promise would stall him for a while. She didn't think that a notarized letter from God would be enough to convince Bill to give up his obsession with the fictitious will.

''See that you do,'' Bill snarled and then slammed the phone down.

''Who was that?''

She turned at the sound of Lucas's voice to find him watching her with an alert expression that made her very nervous. Had the hectoring sound of Bill's voice carried to where Lucas was? Or was he simply making conversation?

''Just a friend.'' It was odd, she thought unhappily. She didn't mind in the least lying to Bill. But she hated the necessity of even shading the truth with Lucas. She wasn't sure if it was because Lucas was such an ethical man himself or if it was because she was head-over-heels in love with him. But whatever the reason, she hated lying to him.

''What was that about poor old Percy being part pit bull?''

''It was a joke,'' she improvised. ''Nothing important. If we're going into town, let's get going.''

Lucas studied her pale features for a long moment, feeling his frustration grow. That hadn't been any friend she'd been talking to. Or, more accurately, listening to. She hadn't really contributed that much to the conversation except for that piece of fiction about Percy. Almost as if she were trying to dissuade someone from coming out here. But who?

He didn't think she was seeing anyone. She certainly hadn't mentioned anyone before and, for that matter, when would she have found the time for a man in her life? They'd been working horrendous hours since August.

And her body language hadn't been that of someone talking to a lover. His eyes narrowed thoughtfully. She'd been tense throughout the whole conversation. Almost as if she were afraid.

Anger shot through him. Who had dared to threaten her? And what were they threatening her with? Certainly not her past.

Not only had his cousin Emmy given her a glowing personal recommendation but he'd had her very thoroughly investigated before he hired her. Her life to that time had been blameless to the point of boredom. And ever since he'd hired her, she hadn't had the time to get into any trouble.

Impotent frustration filled him. So much was at stake, and he not only didn't know the rules of whatever game she was playing, he didn't even know all the players.

''Lucas?'' Jocelyn asked uncertainly, worried about the emotions she could see flitting across his face but couldn't read. Clearly he had some doubts about her explanation of the phone call—doubts she had no way of alleviating without causing yet more complications.

''Sorry.'' Lucas forced his worries to the back of his mind. ''I was just trying to imagine Percy in the role of a pit bull. It boggles the imagination. I'd sooner see Max as vicious.''

Jocelyn relaxed slightly at Lucas's tone of voice. She followed his gaze to the pair of animals. Max was snuggled next to Percy fast asleep.

"One of my foster mothers used to say to be wary of the quiet ones, 'cause they were the most dangerous. Of course, she was the one who had also told me that God would strike me dead if I told a lie, and I proved that one wrong."

"That's a hell of a thing to tell a kid." Lucas was outraged. "What was she trying to do, give you nightmares."

Jocelyn chuckled. "Nothing so devious. She just wanted me to be truthful."

"So she lied to you?" Lucas asked incredulously. "What kind of idiot was she?"

"Actually she wasn't all that bad," Jocelyn said reflectively. "She was just an overworked housewife trying to make ends meet by taking in foster kids."

"How many foster homes were you in?" Lucas asked.

"Far more than I wanted to be in. Shall we go?" she said, changing the subject.

"I take it you don't like talking about your years in foster care?" Lucas persisted in the face of her dismissive tone. She was the one who'd claimed to be married to him, and when she'd done that she'd given him the right to ask personal questions.

Jocelyn stared out the patio window at the wren perched on the deck railing and examined her feelings.

"No, it's not that exactly. It's that it doesn't seem relevant anymore," she said, struggling to explain. "It's like it was a different life. A life that happened to someone else and doesn't have anything to do with me."

Lucas gave in to the impulse to take her in his arms. He gathered her close to his chest and nestled his face into the flowery fragrance of her hair. She smelled so delectable. No matter what else happened, she would always remind him of spring. Of new beginnings.

"That's because you're an adult now and no longer dependent on the system."

"Or a captive of it." Jocelyn relaxed into him, greedily hoarding the unaccustomed sensation of being comforted.

"And you certainly won't make those mistakes on our kids," he said, and her heart skipped a beat at the very thought of their having kids.

"No, I'll probably make a whole new set of mistakes," she said, forcing herself to respond lightly. "And pleasant as it is to dally with you, we need to get going."

"Dally?" Lucas turned her slightly so he was looking down into her eyes. "Is that what this is, dallying?"

"It's as good a word as any," she muttered.

"Oh, no. I can think of much better words."

"You can?" Jocelyn felt her breathing constrict at the sensual glow building in his eyes.

"Definitely. Let me see." He pretended to contemplate the idea. "I think one of my favorites is *kiss.*"

"Kiss?" she muttered.

"Like this." His mouth closed over hers.

A tremor of reaction shot through her, sending shivers coursing over her skin. Before she could properly enjoy the sensation he lifted his head and continued, "And there's *kiss*'s close cousin *nuzzle.*"

He lowered his head and explored the spot behind her left ear with his lips. Jocelyn jumped at the sensation, and his arms tightened.

"That's quite a family!" Her voice came out on a breathless squeak.

Satisfied, Lucas dropped his arms and stepped back. Whatever else was going on, she wasn't indifferent to him physically. She liked it when he kissed her. He was positive of it.

''As you said, time's a-wasting. We need to get into town and get the rest of those Christmas lights before someone else beats us to them.''

''Christmas lights,'' she repeated as she struggled to pull her competent professional persona around her. She couldn't. The best she could come up with was a semi-competent helper. One who was in eminent danger of losing her head over Lucas. The thought sobered her. This wasn't going to last. As soon as he regained his memory, she would be gone. Probably gone with his condemnation ringing in her ears. She had to keep some mental distance between them or the pain would be all the worse.

But how, she wondered. How was she supposed to do that when he kept touching her?

## Chapter Ten

Jocelyn raised her eyebrows at the colored sugars Lucas was dropping into their grocery cart.

"Red and green are the usual colors one associates with the season," she said.

She picked up a container of pale-violet-colored sugar and studied it. "This looks like it was left over from last Easter."

"Sugar keeps," he said as he watched her expressive features. "It'll still be good come spring."

Which was more than could be said of her, he thought grimly. She'd be gone by spring. Would be gone by Christmas if he admitted to having regained his memory. So why didn't he just do it and get it over with? he wondered. Why drag the parting out? Because he wanted to know her motivation for her impersonation. He refused to delve any deeper than that.

Besides, this would give him a chance to do all sorts of things he normally couldn't or shouldn't do. Like kissing her. His eyes dropped to her delectable lips, and a curl of anticipation unfurled in him. Not knowing any better absolved all kinds of behavior.

''Although, this blue is very pretty, particularly next to the bright pink.'' She turned the container to one side the better to study the hue.

Lucas watched her slender fingers grip the container wishing they were touching him. Wishing her fingers would caress his body. Wishing…

He blinked as he suddenly realized something. He knew she wasn't wearing either an engagement ring or a wedding ring because she wasn't married to him. But he wasn't supposed to know that. Surely a man who thought he was married to a woman would ask why she didn't have on a ring?

And her answer might give him a clue as to what she was planning. If she jumped at the chance to get an expensive ring out of him…

''You aren't wearing any rings,'' he said. ''Why not?''

Jocelyn looked up from her study of the various sugars, caught off guard by his totally unexpected words. She could hardly tell him the real reason she wasn't wearing rings.

Which left yet another lie. But which lie? she wondered. Should she him she had taken them off and…

And what? Left them somewhere? Lost them? That hardly sounded like a wife who loved her husband, and she did love him, even if he wasn't her husband.

''We got married rather suddenly,'' she improvised, ''and never got around to buying rings.''

''Well it's time we did.'' Lucas started pushing the cart toward the checkout line. ''I want everyone to know that you're my wife.''

''We can see to it once we get home,'' Jocelyn said, trying to stall.

"They don't have jewelry stores in Vermont?"

"That's not the point."

"Then what is?" Lucas demanded. Perversely, the more she tried to talk him out of it, the more determined he was to do it.

"You don't remember me. Not really. Wedding rings should be bought by people who are sure of what they are doing and with whom they're doing it," she said, struggling to come up with a reason he might accept.

"Okay, I'll compromise. No wedding ring until I get my memory back. We'll just get an engagement ring. Unless you're ashamed to tell the world we're committed to each other?" he said.

"Oh, no!" The unmistakable sincerity in her voice startled him. She sounded as if she really liked him. But if she really liked him then why the hell was she leaving him? A sudden flash of pain sliced through his head at the paradox. Nothing about this whole situation made any sense, and it was really starting to get to him. If it was the last thing he did, he was going to get to the bottom of it.

"What's wrong?" she asked urgently when she saw him wince.

"Just a twinge of pain," he said honestly. "It's gone now. Come on, let's get this stuff paid for." He started loading their supplies onto the checkout conveyer.

Jocelyn helped him, grateful at least that she had talked him out of buying a wedding ring. She just wished she'd been as successful with the engagement ring. It was going to be very painful to wear his ring for a few days and then have to give it back.

Lucas took the receipt for the groceries that the clerk handed him, shoved it in the pocket of his jeans and started pushing the cart toward the door.

Jocelyn followed him out of the store, shivering as the bitter wind pounced on her.

"Bet we have snow later on." Lucas gestured toward the heavy gray clouds that loomed overhead.

"Kind of looks like it, doesn't it? We can check the local weather once we get the radio you bought plugged in."

"Wait till I get that satellite dish installed and the television hooked up," he said as he began to load the groceries into the trunk. "Then we can track the storms."

"Once I get the satellite dish installed," she corrected. "You are not going up a ladder."

"Ha!" Lucas looked down his nose at her. "Women don't know anything about construction. It's always a man who does the remodeling on those old houses they show on television. What does that tell you?"

"That sex discrimination is alive and well on the airwaves?"

She handed him the last bag of groceries.

"You might have a point," he considered, "but only a minor one. It takes muscles to heft lumber and heavy equipment."

And Lucas had muscles. Jocelyn shivered as she remembered the feel of those muscles as she'd snuggled up next to him while he'd slept. Lucas had fantastic muscles.

"Do you know anything about construction?" he asked. "For that matter, do I know anything about it?"

"The extent of my building knowledge is how to replace a lightbulb, and I haven't a clue about you. I've never seen you do anything like that."

"I don't think we need to worry. That salesman said that an eight-year-old could install the dish," Lucas said.

"That is not comforting. The average eight-year-old can run rings around any adult when it comes to operating electronic equipment. I have a friend who swears that her ten-year-old daughter is the only one who can work their VCR."

"Come on." Lucas took her arm and started across the grocery store parking lot toward the shops that lined the street.

"Where are we going?" she asked.

"I told you. We're going to get you an engagement ring."

"I still think we should wait till we're back in Philadelphia." She tried one more time to stall. "They have much bigger stores there."

"No," Lucas said succinctly. "I want to buy one now."

Jocelyn lapsed into silence, not knowing what else to say. Flatly refusing to go along with this would worry him and stress him out.

She bit her bottom lip in frustration. At the rate things were going, she was the one who was going to be suffering from an overdose of stress. And it would reach critical proportions once Lucas regained his memory and found out what she'd done.

Maybe she should pretend to suddenly feel faint and ask to go home? No, not faint. Lucas would insist on driving. Maybe...nauseous. That was it, she decided. Once they were in the store she would claim she felt queasy and tell him they could get the ring the next time they were in town. Then all she had to do was to make sure there was no next time.

Lucas paused in front of the shop windows to study their displays while Jocelyn tried to decide if she should pretend to be ill now or wait until they were actually inside. She glanced around the street looking for an inspiration and then froze when she caught sight of the dark man loitering across the street. Surely that wasn't...

It was! Her heart plummeted and her stomach twisted painfully as she recognized him. What was Bill doing stalking them? Dumb question, she answered herself. He was trying to increase the pressure on her. Not that it was necessary. A little more pressure and she had the scary feeling she was going to crack. For the first time in her life she truly understood that old saying about having a tiger by the tail. And there was nothing she could do about it.

There was no appeal that she could make to Bill that would suddenly turn him into a decent human being. And there was no way she could suddenly wave a magic wand and restore Lucas's memory to him so that he could deal with Bill. And even if she could do that, she didn't want to, she conceded honestly. She wanted these few days with him. Needed them to build an emotional bulwark against what promised to be a lonely future.

When Bill smirked at her, she hastily placed herself between Lucas and the sight of his half brother.

"Let's go check this place out." Lucas opened the door to the jewelry shop.

She was as eager now to go inside as she had been to avoid the place minutes ago.

"May I help you?" The bored-looking pudgy man leaning on the counter suddenly straightened up at the sight of them.

"Yes, we want to see some engagement rings," Lucas said.

Turning to Jocelyn, Lucas said, "I like something with a little color to it. What about you?"

"Zircons are nice and they're hard to distinguish from

the real thing if you aren't an expert,'' Jocelyn said in a last-ditch effort to get him to change his mind.

Instead, what she got was two sets of disapproving male eyes focused on her.

''Real stones are an excellent investment,'' the salesman told her.

''But suppose I lose it?''

''We'll insure it,'' Lucas said.

Jocelyn stifled a sigh. She had the odd feeling that she'd completely lost control of the situation. Not that she'd ever had total control to begin with. But for whatever reason, the upper hand had shifted to Lucas, and she didn't know why. Unless it was the fact that his natural personality was coming more and more to the fore as time passed. And there was no denying that Lucas was a forceful man used to getting his own way.

Jocelyn glanced over her shoulder to check on Bill's whereabouts and discovered him right outside the window. Her stomach lurched. Damn the man! Was he nuts? Even given that he was trying to scare her into cooperating with him, common sense should tell him not to let Lucas see him. But then from what she'd seen, Bill and common sense didn't even have a nodding acquaintance.

''Just a moment while I get our better rings out of the safe.'' The salesman hurried into the back.

''Do you want yellow gold or white?'' Lucas asked.

''Umm.'' Jocelyn struggled not to glance over her shoulder again.

''Don't look so worried. I can afford it. You told me I could afford to buy anything I wanted, and I want to buy the woman I love an engagement ring.'' Lucas said the words, secure in the knowledge that he could say them without any consequence. All he had to do was claim he had only said he'd loved her because he'd thought he was married to her.

"I like yellow gold," she finally said.

"Here we are." The salesman bustled back. He set down a tray of engagement rings on the counter and rubbed his hands together rather like a pudgy genie about to perform some magic.

"Now what kind of stone did you folks have in mind?"

Jocelyn started to say small, but Lucas got in first.

"Something like this one is nice." He picked up a rose diamond that looked to be a good two carats. "It's pretty, and it's set in yellow gold.

"Unless you'd prefer something with more color to it?" Lucas asked.

Jocelyn swallowed the lump in her throat as she looked at the delicate beauty of the exquisite ring Lucas was holding.

"It has plenty of color," she said. "A lovely pinkish hue. Like the sunrise in summer."

"Do you like it?" He sounded hesitant, and Jocelyn rushed to reassure him.

"I think it's absolutely gorgeous, but it also must be..."

She glanced uncertainly at the hovering clerk.

To her surprise, the man not only realized the reason for her hesitation, but tried to help. "We have a similar rose diamond in a slightly different setting that might appeal to you more." He held up a ring that was about one-fourth the size of the one Lucas had picked out.

"No!" Lucas said emphatically. The more she tried to talk him out of it, the more determined he was to buy it. "I like this one. Try it on."

Jocelyn held her breath as he slipped it on her finger.

"It's a perfect fit," he said in satisfaction. "And it looks gorgeous on you."

Jocelyn stared down at it through the tears in her eyes. She wanted so much for this to be true that her chest ached.

"Jocelyn?" Lucas noticed the tears glistening on her eyelashes, completely confused by her reaction. She should have grabbed the ring with both hands. His stepmother certainly would have. But Jocelyn had not only tried to talk him out of it, she looked about ready to cry once he'd succeeded in forcing it on her. He didn't understand any of this, and it made him feel faintly frantic.

"If you really don't like that one..."

"I love it." Her voice came out muffled from trying to control her emotions. "It's absolutely perfect."

Lucas took her in his arms and gently placed a kiss on her lips. "Then it's yours."

"Thank you." She gave up the argument. She could always return it once he regained his memory. In fact, she wouldn't have any choice. The return of the ring would undoubtedly be the first thing he'd ask for.

"We'll take it," Lucas told the waiting salesclerk.

"Yes, sir," the clerk said with satisfaction.

As well he should, Jocelyn thought ruefully. It couldn't be every day that someone bought a diamond ring of that size without even pausing to ask the price. She mentally winced at the thought of what it must cost. But precious stones really were a good investment, she told herself. After Lucas regained his memory, he could resell it or something. As long as he never gave it to another woman! A blinding surge of jealousy pulsed through her at the very thought of another woman wearing her engagement ring. It didn't matter that she knew she was being illogical, that under normal circumstances Lucas would never have given it to her. What mattered was that she had accepted with love. In some strange way it was hers and would always be hers, even if she never saw it again once Lucas took it back.

Pulling out his wallet, Lucas extracted his platinum credit card and handed it to the clerk.

''I won't be but a moment.'' The man disappeared into the back again.

''Probably gone to check if the card will take the charge,'' Jocelyn observed.

''I'd have written a check but I don't know how much is in my checking account,'' he said.

''I would expect not enough to pay for this, whatever it is,'' Jocelyn said. ''You're much too smart a consumer to leave that kind of money sitting around in a non-interest-bearing account.''

''Am I?'' Lucas's lips twitched at her earnest expression.

''Most definitely. That's one of the reasons why you're making such a success out of the business. Because you know how to use money.''

But what kind of success was he making out of his personal life? Lucas wondered uneasily. Not only was the woman he wanted poised to leave him, but he couldn't trust her. It was just too bad that emotions couldn't be set in neat rows and added and subtracted logically like numbers could. Then he might have a chance of straightening out this mess. But there was one thing he was becoming more convinced of with each passing hour he spent in her company—Jocelyn was either the greatest actress that had ever lived or she felt something for him. Her response every time he kissed her convinced him of that. But what she truly felt and how deep it went he had no idea.

The clerk came out of the back of the shop again, carrying a credit slip and wearing a slightly apologetic smile. "If I could just see your driver's license, Mr. Forester," he said. "The credit company insists I double-check your identity because of the size of the purchase, you see."

"Certainly." Lucas took out his driver's license and handed it to the man.

The clerk checked the signature against the credit slip and then covertly compared the picture on the license with Lucas.

"That seems to be in order," he said, handing the license back to Lucas. "May I tell you how much I have enjoyed doing business with you both. It is rare to find someone who knows exactly what they want."

Oh, he knew what he wanted all right, Lucas thought grimly. He wanted Jocelyn. He just didn't know if getting her would set him up for a lifetime of being used. An image of his stepmother's discontented features flashed across his mind.

"Thank you," Jocelyn murmured when Lucas didn't reply.

"Do come again," the man urged as they left. "We carry a large line of jewelry for the discriminating buyer."

"I take it that discriminating is a euphemism for expensive," Jocelyn said dryly once they were outside. "May I ask how much this ring cost?"

"No, you may not," he said succinctly. "It is a pledge of my love and a hope for the future. I refuse to put a price tag on something like that."

Jocelyn swallowed the tears clogging her throat. She was finally getting all the words she had ever wanted to hear from Lucas, and he wasn't in his right mind. Life could be very cruel sometimes. Or else it really was totally capricious, and there really was no rhyme or reason to anything that happened. The very thought of such a world made her shiver fearfully.

"What are you looking so somber about?" he asked. "Are you having second thoughts about your choice of ring?"

"No!" All the pent-up longing and frustration she was feeling exploded in that single word.

Lucas was startled by her reaction. He had the odd feeling he was missing something vital, but for the life of him was unable to figure out what it was. In some respects Jocelyn's thought processes were a closed book to him—a book he would give a lot to be able to read. He sighed.

"What's wrong?" Jocelyn caught the soft sigh. "Does your head hurt?"

"No, it doesn't hurt that much anymore. Just an occasional twinge. I was just thinking about Christmas," he lied.

"That's no reason to sigh. Although," she continued thoughtfully, "apparently a lot of people do find the holidays depressing."

"I imagine they could be rather off-putting when everyone and his uncle seems to be part of a happy family and you aren't," Lucas said.

Jocelyn responded to the pain she could hear in his voice by giving him a quick hug. "You have me."

Lucas kissed her. Her lips tasted cold with an undercurrent of warmth that he found intriguing.

"You know what we need to go with our Christmas cookies?" he said as they walked back to the car.

She chuckled. "You mean besides the stereo and the television and the satellite dish and the radio and the DVD player?"

"Those are simply necessities of modern life. I was referring to another Christmas tradition. We need a tree."

"A tree?" Jocelyn repeated.

"A real one that smells of pine."

"And drops pine needles all over the carpet?" she said.

"All part of Christmas." He dismissed the inconvenience.

"There speaks a man who has never run a sweeper in his life!"

Lucas grinned at her. "That's slander. And I'd prove it if I could remember my past. As it is, you'll just have to take my word for it."

"Forget words, I want deeds!"

"Oh." Lucas's lips formed a sensual smile that sent her heartbeat into overdrive. "You were the one who put the moratorium on our sex life."

Which didn't make a whole lot of sense, either, he suddenly realized. Even if the doctor really had said no sex, which he doubted, chances were extremely good that it wouldn't have hurt him. And her getting pregnant would mean that, even if she couldn't convince him to marry her, she would have both a legal and a moral drain on his wallet for the next eighteen years. And yet she hadn't done it. Why?

"The deed I was asking for was you running the sweeper to pick up the pine needles that fall," she said in a slightly breathless voice.

"It's a deal," Lucas promptly accepted. "We'll stop at that garden center we passed on the outskirts of town and get a tree and all the junk one puts on it."

"You'd better have the tree delivered," she said. "The ornaments we just might squeeze into the car."

"I don't know if they deliver, and besides I don't want to wait that long," Lucas said. "We'll tie it to the roof of the car. You should have let me get a minivan."

''At the rate you seem bent on acquiring things, a full-size pickup truck would make more sense,'' she said.

''All right,'' Lucas gave in. ''In the meantime we'll just have to make do with the Mercedes.'' He inserted his key in the car's lock and opened the door for Jocelyn.

''Make do?'' Jocelyn muttered with a look around the luxurious interior. Most people could never afford something like this and he talked about making do with it? Sometimes she didn't understand Lucas at all. All the money he had, all the money he made and it didn't seem to matter to him. She had the feeling that he'd be exactly the same man if he didn't have a penny to his name. The essential part that was Lucas Forester was not tied up in his financial worth. Not in his own mind and not in hers. He…

The sun peeping out from behind the heavy cloud cover shot through the windshield, illuminating her hand. Her ring seemed to gather the sun's rays to it, returning it in a rainbow of colors.

Her breath caught in her throat at the beauty of it.

''What the matter?'' Lucas asked as he slipped into the passenger seat.

''My ring. Look.'' She moved her hand to intensify the phenomenon. ''Isn't it fantastic?''

''Yes,'' Lucas agreed, his eyes on the hand wearing the ring. She had such capable hands. Capable and competent and beautiful. It was her mind he couldn't seem to get a handle on.

Jocelyn looked across at him, and her breath caught in her throat at the expression on his face. He looked so confused. Unable to resist the impulse, she leaned across the wide seat and kissed him and then hastily retreated as the fact of her actually instigating a kiss registered.

"Thank you, wife." He gave her a smile that made her feel as if she had just won the lottery.

"To the garden center," he said.

"To the garden center." She started the car and pulled out of the lot. "But I want you to sign an indemnity paper for any damage that tree might cause to the roof of the car once we get home. I intend to wave it at you if the car rental people want a new paint job."

"Your wish is my command." Lucas relaxed back against the seat, feeling at peace with the world. He knew it was illogical, because he still didn't have a clue as to what was going on. But despite that, he was happy. He was out with Jocelyn and, when they were done shopping, they would go home. Home to Percy and Max. Before, the lodge had simply been a place to stay while he went skiing. Something a little more convenient than a hotel room. But Jocelyn's presence had changed all that. Now it was a refuge from the world. A welcoming place.

Their stop at the garden center was enormously successful. Lucas picked out a nine-foot tree and then proceeded to fill one of the garden center's carts with lights and glittery bulbs and garlands. He even had to hold a couple of the bags of bulbs on his lap on the trip home because the rest of the car was stuffed to capacity.

Jocelyn slowly pulled into the driveway of the lodge and gently applied the brakes. "Thank heavens we made it," she muttered. "I kept having this horrible feeling that if I had to hit the brakes, the tree would shoot off the roof over the hood and we'd crash into it."

"I tied that tree down myself."

She grinned at him. "Like I said, I kept having this fear..."

"Next year, you can do it." He carefully shifted his

bags of ornaments as he got out of the car. Jocelyn grabbed a couple of bags from the back seat and followed him.

"You leave it up to me, and I'll buy an artificial one," she said.

Lucas shuddered. "Philistine."

He turned and looked back at the car. "You know," he said slowly. "You don't tend to realize how big a nine-foot tree is until you put one on your car."

Jocelyn followed the direction of his gaze. He was right. That was an awful lot of tree.

"We still have to untie it and carry it into the house. And then we have to set it up," she said.

"Worse comes to worst, we can drag it inside. And setting it up won't be a problem. That tree stand we bought said anyone can do it."

"If you believe that, I've got a bridge I want to sell you." She took the bags from him while he opened the front door.

"You can sell me anything." He grinned at her.

"I'll remember that." She flushed slightly at the sensual expression in his eyes.

"Where are the animals?" she asked.

"Right where we left them." Lucas pointed to the dog bed. Percy and Max were huddled in it, eyeing them cautiously.

"The poor little dears." Jocelyn hurried over to them. "They look like they expect us to turn into monsters in front of their eyes."

"A not unreasonable assumption considering what their last owner did," Lucas said grimly. He followed her over and crouched down beside her in front of the animals. "I imagine it's going to take a while before they come to trust us."

He reached out and gently scratched behind Percy's ears while Jocelyn stroked Max and murmured soothingly to the pair.

"Why don't I take Percy for a quick walk outside before we unload the car?" Lucas said.

"Look how his ears perked up when you said *outside.*" Jocelyn patted Percy encouragingly. "He clearly recognizes the word."

"He's a very bright little dog. Let's go, boy." Lucas stood up, and Percy bounded out of his bed.

"I'll..." She broke off as her cell phone which she'd left on the coffee table suddenly rang. Her heart plummeted. It was probably Bill. It was inconceivable that he would see her in town and not call to make some more demands.

She licked her dry lips, not wanting to answer it but also not wanting to ignore it and make Lucas suspicious.

"Here." He reached over, picked up the phone and handed it to her.

Jocelyn held it up to her ear, took a steadying breath and muttered, "Hello?"

# Chapter Eleven

Relief flooded through Jocelyn when she heard the deep voice of Lucas's vice president answer her greeting.

''Richard, what may I do for you?'' she asked.

Lucas frowned, wondering what Richard wanted. The company should be running on automatic with the holidays so close. He briefly considered listening to Jocelyn's end of the conversation and then decided that he wasn't all that interested. If it was something important, Jocelyn would tell him about it, but at the moment he had more important things to do. There was the car to finish unloading, the electronic equipment to set up and the tree to decorate.

He felt a sense of satisfaction. The day was shaping up just the way he'd planned.

He had dragged the tree into the living room, leaving a trail of pine needles across the carpet, brought the electronic equipment in and was almost through unloading the trunk when Jocelyn came outside to help him finish.

"That was Richard," she told him as she picked up a sack of groceries.

"Oh?" Lucas took the last bag, slammed the trunk closed and followed her into the house. "Did he want anything in particular or was he just checking in?"

"In particular." Jocelyn carried the bag of groceries into the kitchen. "He said that the owner of Metron called him this morning."

"Metron?" Lucas repeated absently as he started to put all the butter they'd bought into the refrigerator. He frowned as he stacked it in a neat pile on the bottom shelf. He still thought they should have gotten more. Five pounds didn't seem like that much for cookies.

Assuming his abstracted tone was because he didn't know who Metron was, Jocelyn added, "They make the electronic circuits for some of the items you manufacture. You tried to buy them last year, and David Wilson, the owner, refused. According to Richard, Mr. Wilson called this morning and said that he and his wife have decided to sell the company and retire while they're still young enough to do the things they've always wanted to do.

"So he's giving you first refusal on the company. Richard doesn't know what to do. He knows you want it, but he doesn't feel he can make them an offer without your signing off on it first. Plus, he's not sure how high you're willing to go to get it."

Lucas felt a momentary flash of pleasure at the realization that he would finally be able to buy Metron. But his pleasure quickly ebbed at the thought that if he bought it, he'd have to run it. He'd have to deal with the day-to-day problems that would inevitably come up. He wouldn't own Metron, Metron would own him. Or, more accurately, it would own a big chunk of his time.

Slowly Lucas put the colored sugars away in the cabinet as he considered the idea. He didn't really want to invest a lot of time in yet another company, he realized with a slight sense of shock. He didn't want to take on anything else that would eat into his free time. He'd much rather spend that time with Jocelyn. Because he loved her; he could no longer deny the reality of his feelings. He was in love with a woman whose motives were a complete mystery to him.

"Richard called to ask me what I thought," Jocelyn continued.

Lucas made a monumental effort to sound normal. This wasn't the time to make her suspicious. Besides, the fact that he had these feelings for her didn't really change anything, he told himself. If their relationship was ever to have the slightest chance of developing into anything worthwhile, he had to find out why she was pretending to be his wife and why she'd so abruptly resigned. He wouldn't be like his father, he thought grimly. He wouldn't allow a greedy, grasping woman to use his love to control him.

"What did you tell him?" Lucas asked.

"I told Richard I'd talk to you."

"I don't feel any burning urge to buy anything called Metron," he said.

"But you don't feel *any* burning urges at the moment," Jocelyn said in frustration. She'd always prided herself on being the type of administrative assistant who was up for anything. But nothing she had learned in either school or the business world had prepared her to deal with a situation like this.

"Oh, I wouldn't say that." Lucas's deep voice sent shivers through her. "My urge to make love to you borders on incendiary."

Jocelyn flushed, wishing with all her heart that he really

meant it and wasn't just conditioned to think he should make love to her because he thought they were married.

"Be serious," she muttered. "This is business."

"A singularly boring subject next to the idea of making love to you," he said.

"What should I tell Richard about Metron," she said more to herself than to him.

"Tell him I'm not interested in acquiring Metron," Lucas said as he began to stash the rest of his cookie-making supplies in the cabinet.

"Today you aren't," Jocelyn conceded. "But who knows about tomorrow. You could regain your memory at any time and then what?"

"I think I'll manage to live beneath the crushing blow of not getting them." And it was true, he realized. No matter what happened between him and Jocelyn, one thing his accident had taught him was that there was more to life than just work.

Jocelyn studied him uneasily. Lucas had sounded very emphatic when he'd said that. Very normal. The problem was that while his tone was normal, what he was saying wasn't. The entire time she'd known him, his whole focus had been on expanding his company. On growing. On being the biggest and the best in his field. It made no sense that a temporary loss of memory could produce a complete reorientation of his priorities. And for that matter, what were his new priorities? she wondered. At the moment they seemed to consist of creating holiday memories. And he was doing a good job of it.

A smile curved her lips at the thought of all the decorations he was putting up. He brought the same intensity to having fun as he did to business. Would he bring that same intensity to making love? Her breath caught in her throat at the thought.

"I don't know what to do," she finally said.

Lucas took her in his arms, pulling her close to his chest. "You can quit worrying is what you can do."

He pressed his face into her hair. It smelled delicious. Like ripe peaches in the summer sun. He moved his head slightly so that he could nuzzle the skin behind her ear.

"Neither you nor Richard has the authority to do anything, anyway," Lucas said, wanting to dispose of the subject of Metron once and for all.

He felt her tense slightly in his arms. "How do you know that?" she asked.

Careful, Lucas told himself. Don't make her suspicious.

"You've already said that I own the company outright. Therefore, it makes sense that I would be the only one who could make that kind of decision. And, since I didn't expect to have the accident, I certainly wouldn't have made provisions for a transfer of power."

"No, I guess not," Jocelyn said slowly, having the unsettling feeling that she was missing something important but unable to figure out exactly what. Then Lucas's warm lips trailed over her cheek and found her mouth and she ceased to think at all and simply felt.

Her heart began to race, and there was a ringing in her ears that...

Ringing? That was her cell phone.

"Damn!" Lucas's expletive echoed her feelings exactly.

"I'd better answer it," she said reluctantly. "It's probably Richard calling back to find out what you had to say."

"Tell him I don't want it." Lucas reluctantly released her and followed her out into the living room hoping to resume the kiss once she'd gotten rid of her caller.

"How about if I tell him to stall instead?" she said.

"To talk to them, but not to commit to anything? Then when you regain your memory, you can make your own decisions."

"Okay, just hurry up. We have a lot to do."

Jocelyn smiled at him as happiness surged through her. The things they had to do were simple things, but they meant so much when done with a person you loved. The only way it could be better would be if she and Lucas really were married and, after they'd finished, they could light a fire and make love in front of it.

Jocelyn answered the phone. Expecting to hear Richard's deep bass tones, it was a decided shock to hear Bill's high-pitched whine.

"I found out what you're up to," Bill said.

Jocelyn cast a surreptitious glance at Lucas. To her relief he was taking the tree stand out of the box.

"And what's that?" she asked.

"Don't play coy with me, babe. I saw what you conned out of old Lucas in that jewelry store. You're using the situation to get everything you can out of him. The only difference between you and me is that I think big."

Jocelyn swallowed nervously. It sounded as if Bill knew that Lucas had lost his memory, but how?

Don't panic and above all don't volunteer any information, she told herself. Bill could be guessing. Hoping to surprise her into a damaging admission.

"You meet me in town in half an hour, and I'll tell you what you're going to do," Bill ordered.

"I'm not sure..."

"I am." The gloating sound in Bill's voice sent her anxiety level through the roof. "I'll be at that restaurant across from the drugstore on Main Street. Don't put me to the trouble of coming after you." He slammed the phone down.

Jocelyn stared down at the beige carpeting as she tried to think, but she couldn't get past the self-satisfaction she'd heard in Bill's voice. He was very sure of himself, but the question was, why? Did he really know that Lucas had lost his memory or was he referring to something else? And if it was something else, then what else?

Damn! she thought in frustration. There wasn't a single part of this whole mess that she had a handle on. Not even her own emotions.

She stole a quick glance out of the corner of her eye at Lucas. What excuse could she give him to go back into town when they'd just spent the whole morning there? Keep it general, she finally decided. Generalities were harder to counter.

Jocelyn rubbed her head, which was beginning to ache with the tension gripping her, took a deep breath and said, "I have to go back into town. I forgot to get something at the drugstore."

She watched as Lucas looked up from his unpacking of the Christmas ornaments and gave her a narrow look, which made her very nervous. Just because he'd lost his memory didn't mean he'd lost his normal intelligence.

"You want to go all the way back into town?" he repeated, wondering who had been on the phone to upset her so. And she was upset. He could almost see the tension radiating from her. It couldn't have been Richard again. Her response to his call had been simple frustration at not knowing what to do. But this phone call...

Lucas stared into her shadowed eyes. She was afraid of something or someone. He felt a surge of anger that he struggled to keep hidden. He wanted to smash whoever had upset her. To make sure they never bothered her again. But first he had to find out who the person was and what hold they had on her. And he couldn't do that if he stayed behind at the lodge. He had to be on the scene to judge the situation for himself.

"Ok," he said. "I'll come along with you."

"But you were just in town," Jocelyn said, trying to discourage him.

"I want to get a few more ornaments for the tree." He grabbed the first excuse that sounded vaguely plausible. "We didn't have enough room in the car to get everything I wanted. I can do that while you pick up what you want at the drugstore."

Jocelyn saw his determined expression and knew she wasn't going to be able to talk him out of it. Not only wouldn't it work, but he would surely be suspicious if she even tried. And maybe all he really wanted was to get more ornaments. She tried to still her vague fears. It was possible. He had wanted that frightful plastic-Santa lawn ornament that she'd only dissuaded him from buying by pointing out that there wasn't room in the car to get it home. Maybe he was simply using this opportunity to buy it.

"Fine," she agreed, because she really had no choice.

Slipping into her parka, she picked up her purse and headed toward the door, followed closely by Lucas.

The drive into town was accomplished in virtual silence, which increased her sense of impending disaster to stomach-churning proportions.

She felt something akin to relief when they reached the village. All she wanted to do was to get this meeting with Bill over with. To stall him for a few more days to buy time for Lucas to heal.

A feeling of panic chilled her skin, making her feel light-headed at the thought of what it might mean to Lucas's well-being if she couldn't do it.

"Are you feeling all right?" Lucas asked. "You look pale."

"I'm just cold," Jocelyn said. "It's really chilly today."

Lucas didn't bother to point out that while it might be cold outside, inside the car it was pleasantly warm. And had been the entire trip into town.

A surge of impotent frustration filled him. If only he knew what was going on, he'd have a better chance of helping her, but she was hardly likely to confide in him. Not when she thought he still had amnesia. And if he told her he didn't, it would catapult them into a whole different set of problems.

No, he might not like spying on her, but he had to find out what was going on. He had to know if Jocelyn was really just another woman on the make like his stepmother had been.

"How about if I drop you off at the garden center?" Jocelyn said when they reached town.

"Just park in the drugstore lot, and I'll walk to the center. You can pick me up there when you're through."

"All right." Jocelyn pulled into the drugstore parking lot and got out of the car. "I'll be over to get you shortly."

"Take your time," Lucas said. "I want to have a good look at the lawn decorations."

Jocelyn gave him a weak smile before she went into the drugstore. She stopped by a display of cold remedies to the right of the front door so she could watch Lucas out the window. To her relief, he immediately headed down the street in the direction of the garden center.

She let her breath out in a long, relieved sigh. Apparently, all he really wanted was to buy a couple of those plastic monstrosities. The trouble with having secrets you were desperate to keep hidden was that you began to suspect that everyone else was hiding things, too.

She counted to fifty before leaving the drugstore and darting across the street to the restaurant.

Pausing just inside the front door, Jocelyn quickly scanned the almost deserted café. Bill was sitting at a table against the back wall.

Reluctantly she forced her legs to move toward him.

"It's about time you got here," he snarled.

"And a good afternoon to you, too," she retorted, knowing it would be fatal to let him realize just how worried she was.

"I hate being kept waiting, and you'd better not forget it in the future," he snapped. "Now, shut up and sit down."

Much as Jocelyn wanted to hit him upside the head with the hardest thing she could lay her hands on, she forced herself to sit. She couldn't afford the luxury of telling him exactly what she thought of him.

Lucas, from his vantage point in the doorway of the store down the street, watched as Jocelyn left the drugstore and entered the restaurant. Following her, he cautiously peered through the restaurant window, trying to see what she was doing. As he watched, she headed toward the only occupied table in the back.

His guts clenched as he recognized the man sitting there. It was his half brother. Jocelyn was meeting Bill! A red haze of fury momentarily dimmed his vision. The woman he loved had something going on with his half brother. The woman he loved was...

Was what? His intellect fought a battle with the rage pounding through him. Think, Forester, he ordered himself. Don't jump to conclusions.

He moved away from the restaurant window and stared

blindly at the window display of the store next door as he tried to think.

He suddenly remembered something she'd told him while he'd still had amnesia; Jocelyn knew Bill. She'd said she'd met him at a party Emmy had given. And she'd also said she'd dated Bill. The thought left a bitter taste in his mouth. But she'd also claimed to have broken up with him. But if that were true, then why was she meeting him here?

Trying to appeal casual, he inched back in front of the restaurant window and peered in. She was sitting across from Bill, but even from this far away she looked tense enough to break. He gritted his teeth in frustrated anger. What the hell was going on? If she didn't want to be around Bill, and that was certainly what her body language was screaming, then why had she come running when he'd called?

He didn't know, but he was going to find out. Now. The time had passed for playing games. He headed toward the restaurant door.

Inside, Bill grabbed Jocelyn's hand and said, "Gorgeous ring you got out of him, babe."

Jocelyn wrenched her hand away.

"I saw the pair of you going into the jewelry shop and watched through the window. I must say I never would have thought you had so much sense. But tell me, babe, how are you going to get him to marry you before he remembers that you're just his assistant?"

Jocelyn took a deep breath, trying to figure out if he really knew about Lucas's amnesia or if he was just making an inspired guess and was waiting to see how she reacted. It was possible. Bill had raised deviousness to an art form.

"What are you talking about?" she asked.

"I'm talking about the car accident in Buffalo. About you telling everyone there you were his wife. You sure were quick to see the possibilities of the situation."

The admiration in his voice infuriated her, but she knew there was no sense in trying to explain why she'd done it. He wouldn't believe her. In Bill's mind there was no such thing as an altruistic motive.

"How did you find out about the accident?" she asked.

"Richard's secretary told me about it when I called her last night," he said smugly. "It's amazing the things she's told me and all for the price of an occasional dinner and a few vague promises. And once she told me about the accident, it was easy enough to find out the rest."

Jocelyn was torn between pity at the woman's gullibility and anger over her willingness to betray a trust.

"Now this is the way we're going to play it, babe. I'm going to move into the lodge with you and old Lucas and search for the will. It has to be there because it sure as hell isn't anywhere else."

"At this point a rational man might begin to entertain the idea that there isn't a will," she said tiredly.

"There is, I tell you," he hissed. "Dad would never have left the company to Lucas. I was his favorite.

"Anyway, you're going to get him to write me a check for a hundred thousand dollars," he continued.

Jocelyn took a deep breath and said, "No."

He ignored her. "And once I've found the will, I'll fly back to Philly and use the check to stall the more pressing of my creditors."

"No," she repeated doggedly. "I won't do it."

"Listen, babe, there's plenty of money for both of us. If you..."

"No," she repeated for the third time.

"Listen, you bitch—"

Lucas felt almost light-headed with relief as he got close enough to the engrossed pair to hear their conversation. Jocelyn wasn't conspiring with Bill against him. She was trying to shield him from Bill's avarice. But even if she wasn't involved with his half brother, it didn't mean that she loved *him.* The sobering fact dampened his initial elation.

First, he'd get rid of Bill once and for all, and then he'd get to the bottom of her resignation.

''There you are, Jocelyn.'' Lucas's deep voice poured through Jocelyn's mind creating conflicting emotions: fear that a confrontation with Bill might retard his recovery and relief that he was there.

''Why, Lucas!'' Bill gave his half brother a wide smile that wasn't reflected in his eyes. ''The minute I heard about your accident I flew up here to see you. There's a business transaction that simply can't wait, and I need you to write me out a check for a hundred thousand for a deposit so they'll hold the property for us. I was just discussing the problem with Jocelyn. Wasn't I?'' Bill gave her a warning glare.

Jocelyn didn't even consider taking the out Bill was offering her. Much as she wanted to spend even a few more hours with Lucas, she wasn't willing to ally herself with Bill to do it. It would be a betrayal of everything she felt for Lucas.

She swallowed back the tears clogging her throat. She'd always known that her time with Lucas was limited. She just hadn't figured that Lucas would find out what she'd done in a public place.

''You have no business dealings with Bill,'' Jocelyn said flatly. ''He's trying to use your amnesia to steal from you.''

''Lucas, listen to me. I'm your brother,'' Bill broke in.

"I have your best interests at heart. Why do you think I came when I heard about your accident and discovered that your administrative assistant was pretending to be your wife?"

Jocelyn shivered at the expression on Lucas's face. His features looked as if they'd been carved from stone.

"And how did you find out about my accident?" Lucas asked.

"Apparently Richard's secretary thinks she's in love with him and keeps him informed of what's going on," Jocelyn said when Bill didn't say anything.

"I had to come rescue you, brother," Bill said. "I blame myself for your getting mixed up with Jocelyn in the first place. When she found out that our affair wasn't going to result in a marriage proposal—"

Bill's words ended in a strangled gasp as Lucas's large hand closed around the front of his shirt and tightened, cutting off his air supply.

"You've got a few things wrong, little brother."

Jocelyn shivered as Lucas's icy tone seemed to noticeably lower the temperature. "First, I am not suffering from amnesia."

Jocelyn shot Lucas a quick glance, wondering if he was telling the truth. And why hadn't he reacted to Bill's claim that they were lovers? Given his almost paranoid determination not to get involved with women who worked for him, he should have responded to that claim first.

Her eyes seemed glued to the grim set of Lucas's mouth. Unless he was waiting to get her alone before he said anything to her? She shuddered at the thought of the confrontation yet to come.

"But she said..." Bill sounded confused. "You have to be. Otherwise why did you buy Jocelyn that huge diamond? And why are you still up here instead of flying back to Philly and negotiating to get Metron?''

''Richard's secretary has been busy, hasn't she?'' Lucas snapped, and Jocelyn felt a flash of pity for the woman. Lucas did not like having his trust violated.

''The second thing you're wrong about is Dad's will,'' Lucas continued. ''While I don't doubt he would have left the company to you if he could have, it wasn't his to dispose of. His leaving it to me in his will was window dressing to try to hide the fact that he didn't own it. Why it would have mattered to him what anyone thought at that point, I don't know. But then, I could never figure out what he saw in you, either.''

''The company was too his!'' Bill insisted. ''Your mother's will left him everything she owned. Mom looked it up before she agreed to marry him.''

''If your mercenary mother had looked a little deeper, she would have found out that my mother never did own the company. My grandfather left it to me in trust when he died. Dad could run it during his lifetime, but once he died it became mine.''

''I don't believe you,'' Bill whispered, his face ashen. ''It can't be true.''

''I don't give a damn whether you believe it or not!'' Lucas's voice would have given an armed man pause. ''I'm going to tell you this once and once only. If you ever come near me or my company again, I'll slap a restraining order on you so fast your head will spin.

''Come on.'' Lucas grabbed Jocelyn's arm and hauled her to her feet.

Jocelyn forced herself to stand when every instinct she had was urging her to run in the opposite direction. Away from the anger she could see seething in Lucas's eyes.

Away from the explanations he was going to demand and wouldn't like once he got them.

But she'd lived her life with the basic philosophy that you make your choices and you pay for them. She swallowed unhappily. She just wished the bill for this particular choice wasn't going to be so high.

"Listen, Lucas." Bill leaned forward, desperate to convince him. "You don't know what you're doing."

Lucas gave Jocelyn a long, complicated look and then looked back at his brother. "You know, I've hated your guts for years, and suddenly I find that it isn't even worth the effort. You're a pathetic parody of a human being."

Without another word, Lucas turned and, still holding Jocelyn's arm in a viselike grip, left the restaurant. Jocelyn tried to throw off the feeling that she was being escorted out under guard, but she couldn't. She felt just like a condemned prisoner, and she hadn't even been given a last meal, the vagrant thought occurred to her, and she almost burst into hysterical laughter.

There was one advantage to this mess, she thought as she struggled to match her shorter steps to Lucas's long stride. She no longer had to worry about what to do. The initiative had been taken out of her hands. Lucas held all the cards. All that remained to be seen was how he was going to play them.

Lucas unlocked the passenger door of the Mercedes, bundled her into the seat and hurried around to the driver's side, almost as if he was afraid she might try to escape.

Once inside the car, he made no effort to start the engine. He simply put his hands on the steering wheel and stared out the windshield.

Jocelyn studied his trembling fingers and shuddered at the evidence of just how angry he was.

"Have you really got your memory back?"

"Yes." He bit the word off.

"For how long?" she whispered.

"Since yesterday morning."

Why hadn't he said something then? she wondered in confusion. Why let her go on thinking he still had amnesia? One look at his uncompromising face made her think better of asking.

"I want an explanation," he finally said.

Jocelyn gulped, trying to figure out where to begin.

She instinctively focused on the thing Bill had said that bothered her the most. "I was never Bill's lover. When I started to date him, he seemed..." She struggled to explain what she'd felt when she'd meet him. "Charming and...I don't know exactly."

"You were attracted to him?" he continued, in that flat voice that sent shivers down her spine.

"I was," she admitted. "We dated for a couple of months, but the more I was around him the more..." She gestured with her hands as if trying to pull words out of the air.

"The more the feeling grew that there wasn't anything there behind his surface charm. We broke up because he wanted to go to bed, and I refused."

Jocelyn held her breath, praying that he would believe her but not really expecting him to.

"Why?" he continued inexorably.

"Because sex isn't a game. It's a deadly serious act that can lead to consequences." She gave a ragged laugh. "Being a consequence myself of one of my mother's casual encounters, I can attest to the problems irresponsible sex causes. I will never, ever risk bringing a child into the world who isn't welcomed by both its mother and its father."

"I see." Lucas felt some of the rigid tension that had gripped him dissipate. What she was saying meshed perfectly with the woman he had come to know over the past six months.

"Bill was waiting for me in the parking lot the day before you got back from your last business trip," she continued. "He said he'd run through the money your father left him, and he started rambling about a missing will. He demanded I help him find it or he'd tell you we were lovers."

"And that's why you resigned? Dammit, Jocelyn!" he snapped, giving vent to his frustration. "Couldn't you have told me what was going on?"

Jocelyn winced at the anger she could hear in his voice. "How could I? When Emmy told me about the job opening as your administrative assistant, she also told me that you were vehemently against getting involved with anyone you worked with. And everyone in the office knew how much you hated Bill. If I told you he was threatening me, you'd find out that I really had dated him and in a sense we did spend the night together and he had the room receipt from the resort to prove it. He tricked me into going to a ski resort with him. But I slept on the couch in the sitting room, and he slept in the bedroom."

She sniffed back the tears that threatened. She absolutely wouldn't cry. It would be too humiliating.

"Why did you pretend to be my wife?" Lucas abruptly switched topics.

"Because I was afraid they'd delay treatment for you until they could locate your next of kin to sign a release. And I wasn't sure whether your stepmother or Bill were listed, but I was sure neither of them would try to help."

"That explains why you did it at the hospital, but why didn't you tell me the truth once we were safely at the lodge? You could have had me talk to Richard. He would have backed up what you told me about Bill."

"The doctor..." Jocelyn started to blame it on the doctor's warning about stress, but the words died on her lips. It wasn't true. Not really. And she'd already told him so many lies. It was time for the truth, no matter how embarrassing she found it. Not only did he deserve to hear the truth, but her own love demanded that she tell it.

"I didn't tell you because...because I love you, and I couldn't pass up the chance to pretend to be your wife for the last few days I'd be with you." She finished in a rush and then stared down at her hands, unable to look at him and see the condemnation in his face. Or even worse, the pity.

"You love me?" he repeated incredulously. "And you resigned!"

"It seemed like my only option," she muttered. "Everyone knows how you feel about getting involved with a woman you work with, and nothing you ever said led me to believe that you'd somehow changed your mind. Actually that was one of the reasons I applied for the job in the first place. Because I figured you wouldn't be chasing me around the desk at work."

Agitatedly Lucas shoved his fingers through his hair. "That attitude is a legacy from my stepmother. But I think my heart has known from the very beginning that you weren't the least bit like her. It just took my head a little longer to figure it out. But then you resigned and I didn't know what the hell to think. If you ever pull a stunt like that again..."

"Does that mean I can have my job back?" Jocelyn said, not sure if it would be a good idea or not. How could she possibly go back to treating him as her boss when she'd spent the last two weeks treating him like her husband? Her beloved husband.

"With certain modifications," Lucas said slowly, almost afraid to put his desires into words for fear of having them rejected.

Taking a deep breath, he blurted out, "I want you as my partner."

"Partner?" she repeated incredulously.

"But you have to marry me first," he finished in a rush, nervously waiting for her answer. She might claim to love him, but that didn't mean she would be willing to marry him. To stay with him and put the effort necessary into building the kind of solid, enduring marriage he wanted.

"Marry you!" Her voice broke on the intensity of her feelings. "But...but why?"

"Why? Because I love you, of course."

Jocelyn heard his words through a daze of joy that momentarily rendered her speechless.

"Jocelyn, I want to make your world perfect. I want to raise a family with you. I want your face to be the first thing I see in the morning and the last thing I see every night. I want your heartwarming smile to be the image I carry to my grave."

"You make my world perfect just by being in it," she said simply. "And I would love to be your wife."

Elated, Lucas started to reach for her and hit his arm on the steering column. The frustrated expression on his face made Jocelyn giggle. She felt light-headed with an intoxicating combination of happiness and relief.

Lucas's entire body clenched at the joyous sound. He felt as if he would explode if he had to wait much longer to kiss her. To taste her. To make her his in every sense of the word.

"Let's go home," he bit the words out impatiently.

"Home?" Jocelyn parroted, totally focused on the tension she could feel pouring off his body.

"Yes, home." Lucas shot her a quick glance, his eyes lingering hungrily on her lips. "So I can show you exactly how I feel about you. I'm a firm believer in that old adage about actions speaking louder than words. I intend to kiss every inch of your tantalizing body, and then I'll work on variations."

The glow in his eyes shortened her breath and made her skin tingle with desire.

"And I'm a very inventive man," he added.

"I can hardly wait." She snuggled deeper into the Mercedes' leather seat as he started the car and swung out into the street. Surely there could be no greater pleasure in this life, she thought as she studied Lucas's beloved profile, than to love and know yourself loved. And to be free to express that love.

* * * * *

# COMING NEXT MONTH

**#1684 LOVE, YOUR SECRET ADMIRER—Susan Meier**
*Marrying the Boss's Daughter*
Sarah Morris's makeover turned a few heads—including Matt Burke's, her sexy boss! But Matt's life plan didn't include romance. Tongue-tied and jealous, he tried to help Sarah discover her secret admirer's identity, but would he realize *he'd* been secretly admiring her all along?

**#1685 WHAT A WOMAN SHOULD KNOW—Cara Colter**
Tally Smith wanted a stable home for her orphaned nephew—and that meant marriage. Enter JD Turner, founder of the "Ain't Getting Married, No Way Never Club"—and Jed's biological father. Tally only thought it fair to give the handsome, confirmed bachelor the first shot at being a daddy…!

**#1686 TO KISS A SHEIK—Teresa Southwick**
*Desert Brides*
Heart-wounded single father Sheik Fariq Hassan didn't trust beautiful women, so hired nanny Crystal Rawlins disguised her good looks. While caring for his children, she never counted on Fariq's smoldering glances and knee-weakening embraces. But could he forgive her deceit when he saw the real Crystal?

**#1687 WHEN LIGHTNING STRIKES TWICE—Debrah Morris**
*Soulmates*
Joe Mitchum was a thorn in Dr. Mallory Peterson's side—then an accident left his body inhabited by her former love's spirit. Unable to tell Mallory the truth, the new Joe set out to change her animosity to adoration. But if he didn't succeed soon their souls would spend eternity apart….

**#1688 RANSOM—Diane Pershing**
Between a robbery, a ransom and a renegade cousin, Hallie Fitzgerald didn't have time for Marcus Walcott, the good-looking—good-kissing!—overprotective new police chief. So why was he taking a personal interest in her case? Any why was *she* taking such a personal interest in *him?!*

**#1689 THE BRIDAL CHRONICLES—Lissa Manley**
Jilted once, Ryan Cavanaugh had no use for wealthy women and no faith in love. But the lovely Anna Sinclair seemed exactly as she appeared—a hardworking wedding dress designer. Could their tender bond break through the wall around Ryan's heart…and survive the truth about Anna's secret identity?